CHRISTMAS LIGHTS

CHRISTMAS LIGHTS

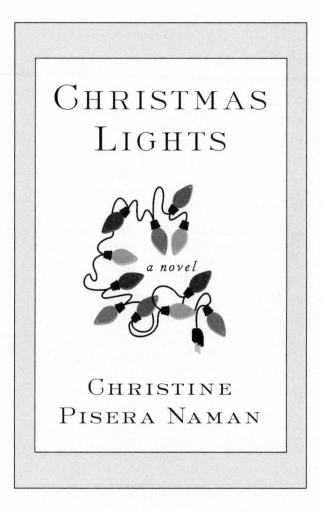

a novel

CHRISTINE PISERA NAMAN

DOUBLEDAY
New York   London   Toronto
Sydney   Auckland

PUBLISHED BY DOUBLEDAY

Published in the United States by Doubleday, an imprint
of The Doubleday Broadway Publishing Group,
a division of Random House, Inc., New York.

www.doubleday.com

DOUBLEDAY and the portrayal of an anchor with a
dolphin are registered trademarks of Random House, Inc.

Book design by Jennifer Ann Daddio

Library of Congress Cataloging-in-Publication Data
Naman, Christine Pisera.
Christmas lights / Christine Pisera Naman.—1st ed.
p. cm.
1. Christmas stories, American. 2. Women—Fiction.
I. Title.
PS3614.A577C48 2007
813'.6—dc22
2006038171

ISBN 978-0-385-52245-8

PRINTED IN THE UNITED STATES OF AMERICA

1 3 5 7 9 10 8 6 4 2

First Edition

KATHERINE

 "I saw my father today," he announced as she entered the room. Startled, she blinked, then rushed toward him, pulling off her heavy winter coat. She quickly dusted off the few flakes of snow that had snuck beneath her coat to attach themselves to her bright red sweater. She sat quickly in the chair next to his walker and gave him her full attention. She knew, of course, that he had not seen his father. He himself was seventy-five years old, and his father had died years before.

She was surprised not so much at what he had said but by how he had said it, a clear competent thought in a complete sentence, even if the thought was an impossible one. Since he had been moved to the dementia floor three years earlier, complete thoughts were fewer and farther between.

She came to see him every day. Most days he was not well and he could not recognize her. But there were those rare days when his eyes held just the slightest glimmer of understanding. And it was those moments of hope that warmed her heart. They seemed to be reserved only for her. Their daughters came and went, visiting regularly, but he showed nothing. His illness had begun slowly, as this type of illness always seems to do, then quickened, until names then faces melted into an unknown past. It had been sad to watch, but she had reminded herself that he had had a good life, a full one, a life full of blessings.

Visiting him wasn't a duty but instead her comfort. She never rushed through her visits but lingered, beginning and ending each with a prayer, just as they had begun and ended each day of their life together. Each day she read a little from the Bible, sometimes reading from his, sometimes reading from hers. The Bibles were tattered now; they had been gifts to one another on their wedding day.

Lately she had had to rely on the flicker that only sometimes appeared in his eyes when she entered the room to know that he still knew her. She had to watch him carefully because that moment disappeared just as quickly as it came.

Often he was silent, offering only a furrowed brow when confronted with even the most basic questions. He didn't know how he was or if he enjoyed lunch or if he thought it was a nice day outside. So, mostly she just talked

To my parents, Frank and Angie, first and always, who made home the happiest, safest place on earth. You filled our home and hearts with love and Christmas Spirit. I remember Biffy the Bear, Baby Secret, and sitting at the Christmas Eve table realizing that I was the luckiest little girl in the world to be your daughter.

To my brothers Rocco and Dan, sister Lisa, nephews Matthew and John, nieces Diana, Marissa, and Nina. I will travel anywhere, no matter how far, to say Merry Christmas to you.

To my husband Peter and children Jason, Natalie, and Trevor, who fill every one of my days with love and blessings. How I ended up so lucky, I will never know. Now we have Game Boys, laptops, and iPods. I wonder what you will remember. Now I sit at the Christmas Eve table realizing that I am the luckiest lady in the world to be your wife and mother.

to him. She told him things. How she was. How their daughters were, how their lives were progressing, their accomplishments and heartaches. She told him about their grandkids and even a bit of gossip about the neighbors. He never offered anything back, but he never acted as if her talking bothered him either, so she just talked on. There was a simple peace in just being together, side by side, just as they had spent the past fifty years. It didn't matter as much as one would think that one of them was no longer who he had been. It was okay because there was a quiet understanding that only people who had nurtured a marriage for fifty years could understand. She tried to explain this to her daughters but was almost sure none of them understood it. She prayed that in time they would understand because when they did, it would mean that they too had successfully grown a marriage. "Fifty years is a lot of lifetime," she would tell them. "Sometimes you walk side by side; sometimes you take turns carrying each other. Together we're still complete."

"So you saw your father?" she tried brightly, shaking the snow from her boots. He had drifted off, but her question brought him back.

"Yes," he answered with the slightest smile, as if savoring the memory. It had been years since he had smiled. His smile had been one of the first things to go. The sight of it warmed her and brought back a flood of old times. For a moment he seemed not so far away.

She decided that it was her Christmas present, a touch of a blessed past. A glimpse of the man she called her husband the way that she wanted to remember him. For some time she had had to struggle to remember him the way he was then instead of the way he had become. But here it had been delivered to her without a struggle like a present, and on Christmas Eve.

So she decided that he too had gotten a Christmas present. Whatever or whoever he had seen, he thought it was his father. And it made him happy. And that was good enough for her.

They spent the rest of the afternoon pleasantly. They chatted in his room for a while. And even though he didn't respond, he seemed to enjoy what she told him. They sampled Christmas cookies and eggnog in the living room. They watched a good bit of *It's a Wonderful Life* in the TV room. She remembered how he loved Jimmy Stewart. "Good, clean, and wholesome," he used to say. "Just like people should be." She encouraged him to make a craft in the group room. But he seemed confused at the idea of gluing rigatoni to cardboard. His Italian blood forbade it, she joked to herself. At three she helped feed him a Christmas dinner of roast turkey, mashed potatoes and gravy, stuffing, cranberry sauce, and pumpkin pie for dessert. His hearty appetite was one thing that never changed.

Finally, they returned to his room. Gently, she stroked the little hair he had left.

"I guess I need to be going, honey," she told him. "I need to get home to prepare Christmas Eve dinner for the girls."

She checked her watch. "I still need to get to Rocco's Deli," she explained. "And pick up the pecan salmon I ordered. It's as good as ever." She knelt down beside him. "Let's pray." Holding his now-frail hands in hers, she recited a prayer. When she was finished, he looked back at her with a childlike innocence. Prayer always seemed to calm him. She felt guilty leaving him. She used to check him out of the nursing home for the holidays and take him home, but the last time she did he almost fell and the time before that he seemed frightened to be in unfamiliar surroundings, so she felt it best to leave him be. It was a decision she always wrestled with.

"Oh my goodness! Your present!" she exclaimed. "I almost forgot to give it to you." She laughed. "It wouldn't be Christmas without a present."

She retrieved the wrapped package from the other side of the room and set it on his lap. He stared straight ahead and made no motion to touch it. She couldn't tell if he even noticed that she had put it there.

"Here. I'll help you open it," she said, guiding his hands to the bow. But when he let his hands fall limp, she tore the wrapping off herself and opened the box.

"It's a quilt," she announced. "See, honey?" She had spent nearly six months making it, beginning in July. "I made it from scraps of all of the girls' old clothing," she pointed out. Bits of dance recital costumes, prom and communion dresses, and graduation gowns all mingled together to form the tapestry. "If you look closely," she promised him, "the years will come flooding back." She hoped so, at least. She held the fabric up, but his eyes didn't follow. He was becoming less and less focused and beginning to drift.

She pressed the blanket to his cheek. "See, it's soft. I thought you would like that." He didn't respond. "Your other one is so tattered." When this comment was met only with silence, she said, "I guess I need to be going."

Her heart, squeezed by sadness and guilt, sank a bit. But, reminding herself that it was Christmas, she forced herself to rally. And with a jolliness that sounded fake even to her she said, "Before I leave, I'll fix you up in your chair with your new quilt and I'll put on your radio."

She led him to the chair across the room. Like an obedient child, he shuffled behind her. She remembered how strong his now-fragile body once had been. She settled him, draping the blanket onto his legs. "It's warmer on this side of the room," she explained. "And this way you'll be close to your radio. You can listen to Christmas music!"

He didn't respond and although she didn't mean to, she sighed. Turning from him, she began gathering her things and putting on her coat.

"There he is," he said. "There's my father."

Startled, she turned. For that split second, his voice was stronger and clearer than it had been in years.

She watched him as a flood of understanding rushed over her. He was staring into the mirror that was anchored to the wall, studying his own reflection. She blinked away a tear as she watched him smile broadly at himself.

"It's good to see him." He chuckled. Cautiously she walked toward him, praying not to disturb the moment. It was like trying to catch a bubble without popping it.

"Yes, it is," she managed softly, reaching him. They peered into the mirror together. Side by side, silently they looked at his image. They stayed that way for several minutes. Dinner could wait.

This time the silence that filled the air was good.

She waited until he had had enough. Finally, she brushed his cheek and kissed him on the top of the head.

"It's good to see him," he murmured again, barely audible, then closed his eyes. He was drifting off to sleep.

She straightened the quilt one last time and stood in the doorway watching him. He slept peacefully with a contented look on his face.

"I'll see you tomorrow, honey," she whispered. "Merry Christmas." She was comforted by noticing that he was gently stroking the quilt as she turned away.

JULIANNA

"This is not worth the service hours," Julianna muttered to herself. "No matter how many it's worth!"

She was chasing what was apparently the fastest four-year-old on the planet through the basement of the church. He was running with scissors. Until that moment, she didn't believe children actually did that. She assumed it was just a cliché. But obviously she was wrong, because there he was running and there she was chasing him. He weaved in and out of every open space between the preschool-size tables and chairs as well as the other preschoolers and teenage volunteers.

"Tyler," she called.

Then, correcting herself, she yelled, "Trevor!"—or was it Travis?

"Oh, crap," she griped to herself. "Stop! Whatever your name is, stop!"

Everyone had been assigned a child. What were the chances of her getting the next Roger Kingdom?

"Please, stop," she whined, finally catching him, only because he had stopped to investigate the train table. She scooped him up, gently took the scissors from his pudgy hand, and began to carry him back to their station.

"You must not run with scissors," she said in her most authoritative yet perky voice, hoping more than anything that the director, Mrs. Armstrong, would hear her using the suggested phrase from the manual they had all been given to study before they arrived. She had read it and signed a statement swearing that she had studied it, which may have been an overstatement but was not exactly a lie.

Julianna considered herself a person who knew a lot about children. After all, it felt as if she had been one forever. Her mother had insisted it was exactly the same sixteen years, 365 days per year that everyone else spent getting to be sixteen, but Julianna disagreed somehow. She was the youngest of six sisters. No one could ever imagine what that was like. To Julianna, her sisters' lives seemed complete and put together while she felt as if she was constantly struggling to put a life together for herself.

As she lugged Trevor (for sure, Trevor; she had

checked his name tag) over to their station, her cell phone beeped with a text message. With a huff, she switched the child from one hip to the other and checked the message.

It read: "Don't forget the salad greens. Be home by 6:00 pm. Love you, Mom."

Julianna rolled her eyes. How many times was she going to remind her? She clicked the phone off. Phones were not permitted to be on when earning service hours, and this job was worth a slew of them and she did not want to jeopardize it. She guessed that most kids thought it was easier to pick up garbage in the park or to sing at the retirement village than it was to chase overexcited preschoolers through the church basement on Christmas Eve day. They were probably right, but truth be told, Julianna liked kids and hoped to have a few of her own someday.

She plopped Trevor down in a tiny chair and herself in the one next to him.

"Let's make Christmas trees," she suggested perkily, squirting glue on top of a cardboard cutout.

"Let's not," he retorted.

"Let's talk nice to each other," she suggested, handing him a shaker of red glitter.

"Let's not," he replied again.

"Let's hope Santa is not hearing you and canceling

your toys," she remarked matter-of-factly, s¡
ver glitter on top of her own cutout.

She watched as Trevor's face went from w
then went off like a siren howling "NOOOOO

Panicking, Julianna tried to silence him. Sh
around self-consciously. The entire room looked

"Shhhhhhhhhhhhhhh," she whispered. "I wa
kidding. He'll still come."

Trevor was having none of it. By this point he
screaming louder and turning purple. Julianna closed
eyes and prayed for patience. When she opened the
what she got instead was a miracle. Well, maybe it wou.
not have been a miracle in anyone else's opinion, but ir
hers it surely was. In the entrance to the basement being
welcomed by the youth group director was Jason Green.
For Julianna he was everything. He was everything that
made a guy wonderful. She liked the way he looked and
walked and talked. But although he may have been
everything to Julianna, he somehow had no idea she was
alive.

Her mother would laugh heartily when Julianna al-
ternately pined about her love for him then pouted about
the fact that he didn't know she was alive.

"Everyone should experience unrequited love at least
once in their life," her mother would say. "It builds character."

"I have enough character," Julianna would protest.

"Impossible," her mother would answer simply.

When she would ask for suggestions as to how she could get his attention, her girlfriends were full of them.

"Send him a card."

"Hang out where he does."

"Go see him play basketball and wave from the stands."

Her mother on the other hand had only one suggestion. "Pray on it."

Julianna had not meant to roll her eyes when she said it, but she had.

"Julianna!" her mother admonished.

Julianna knew it was wrong. "Sorry," she said.

"Not to me," her mother insisted.

Looking heavenward, Julianna said, "Sorry."

She and her mother were in the kitchen of their home when they had this conversation. She was supposed to be helping her mother make Christmas bread, but instead she had plopped onto the kitchen chair with her head down on the table.

"You believe in prayer, of course," her mother pointed out.

"Of course," she agreed.

"So pray on it," her mother said again. "Just a quick one, then move on. If He wants it to be, then He will have

you meet. If He doesn't, then He won't. And in that case, around an unexpected corner there will be another."

This time Julianna hid her rolling eyes by flopping her head onto the kitchen table. Then she popped up.

"God helps those who help themselves," she retorted.

"To a point," her mother conceded. "But for the most part He doesn't need your help."

Giving up and dropping her head back down on the table, Julianna's muffled voice came from beneath the arms that she had curled around her head. "Fine."

"Pray on it. Then let it be," her mother said one last time.

And on that night three weeks ago Julianna had. It hadn't been exactly a quick prayer. She figured if she was going to pray on it only once, she might as well tell Him all that she had been feeling. How she wanted to get to know Him better and how she thought it was right. But she did halfheartedly add that if He thought it was not the right path for her, she would accept that too.

She had promised to accept it, but like it was a different story. In the three weeks since her prayer, she seemed to have become invisible. If she walked in Jason's path, he walked around her. If she waved, he looked beyond her. If she smiled, he smiled at the person next to her. Finally she had given up. She stopped smiling and waving and handed it to Jesus. She gave Him all of it this time.

So for her now to be staring at Jason across the crowded church basement was truly surprising. A shriek louder than the rest from Trevor shook her from her stare.

"Shhhhhhhhhh, listen," she crooned. "I swear I was kidding. Santa is still going to bring you toys."

She was alternating her attention between Trevor seated next to her and Jason and Mrs. Armstrong coming toward her, holding the hand of a cute-as-a-button four-year-old with long blond ringlets. Julianna patted Trevor's back with one hand and ran the other hand through her hair, wishing she had taken more time with it that morning. As they got closer, she pretended to be intently interested in both Trevor and his untouched cutout.

She tracked them out of the corner of her eye, watching them wind their way through the maze of the tables and people coming closer. She glanced around. They were definitely headed her way; there was no room anywhere else. Julianna tried to look busy and focused on her cutout. When they appeared, Julianna looked up and tried to act surprised.

"Here's a spot for you two," the director said brightly. "Jason Green, Julianna Tenley," she introduced. Making timid eye contact, Jason and Julianna greeted each other. Julianna's stomach squeezed, and all of a sudden she wasn't convinced this was such a good idea.

"Amanda, this is Trevor. Trevor, this is Amanda," the director said. Julianna could have kicked herself; she should have jumped in and done that. Trevor had finally calmed down, the arrival of the others distracting him. He was now glaring at Amanda, who had seated herself sedately in the chair next to him. Julianna looked at Jason, who was still standing awkwardly above them. He got the hint and sat down on the other side of Amanda.

The director walked away. Julianna had the oddest urge to run after her, grab her leg like a child, and scream, "Don't leave me alone with him."

She could feel Jason's eyes on her. All of a sudden she was flushed with embarrassment. When she glanced up, there was just a flicker of eye contact.

"Hi," Jason managed self-consciously.

"Hi," Julianna answered, her voice sounding oddly high and thin.

"We go to school together, right?" he asked so timidly it was if he were walking on eggshells.

What Julianna wanted to say was "You've got to be kidding me. I've been dying over you. Eating, sleeping, and breathing you, and you're not even sure if we go to school together." But what she actually said was "Yeah. I think so."

"I know so," he answered.

His reply took her by surprise. And when she looked up at him, he was smiling at her. Not a small subtle smile but a big beautiful smile, the same smile she had seen from a distance and wondered if it would ever shine on her. For a moment it mesmerized her, but then she had to look away. Her mind raced, searching for some sort of witty, alluring reply, but it was blank.

She was just about to say anything. She opened her mouth but instead of her own voice coming out, she heard a horrendous screech from Amanda instead. For a few seconds Jason's and Julianna's only reaction was to stare at her with their mouths open. The sound was the equivalent of a fire truck siren, loud, high-pitched, and long. It was startling that such a huge sound could come out of such a little girl. She sat poker straight, her arms at her sides, and her head tilted slightly upward. Finally, Julianna reacted, jumping from her seat and hurrying to Amanda's side. She began rubbing her tiny back.

"What's wrong? What happened?" she asked. Amanda only screeched louder.

"I can't make it better if you don't tell me what's wrong," Julianna tried, stealing one of her mother's favorite phrases.

"Amanda, tell me what's wrong," she begged, making sure to keep her voice gentle enough to sound kind while still making it loud enough for Amanda to hear over her own howling. The problem was that everyone else in the room heard her too, and pretty much all of them were watching them as if they were watching a really interesting television show.

"Tell me honey, please," Julianna begged. Finally

Amanda gave her a clue by motioning her howl toward Trevor.

"Trevor?" Julianna guessed, as if she were playing charades. "Did Trevor do something to you?" Now Amanda added head bobbing to her screaming.

"Trevor, what did you do?"

"What did Trevor do to you?" she asked Amanda. The screaming got even louder, although if anyone had asked Julianna a minute earlier, she would have said that was not possible. Amanda now clutched her left arm.

"Did you hit her, Trevor? Did he hit you?" Amanda responded to this with louder screaming.

"Trevor hit you in the arm?" Julianna stated, solving the puzzle. Amanda was now nodding up and down frantically while she continued to holler.

"Trevor, why would you do that?" Julianna asked him incredulously.

Trevor's response was to position his back poker straight, put his arms down at his sides, turn his head slightly upward, and scream.

"Oh, brother," Julianna grumbled, shaking her head back and forth, not believing her rotten luck.

What a sight they were, two four-year-olds sitting side by side, in identical positions, screeching to the high heavens. Jason was still frozen. As he looked at her pleadingly, his eyes seemed to say "Please fix this."

Julianna looked at his frightened face and almost felt

bad for him. Then she grinned. It *was* all a little funny, she realized, looking from Jason to the children. She laughed, then said to Jason, "You can laugh. It's kind of funny."

His face relaxed and he looked at the children, then at her, and laughed too. "It is kind of funny?" he said. His words sounded somewhere in between a statement and a question. Julianna nodded and chuckled. They were incredibly cute children, even in this condition. For another second they smiled together, then, catching sight of Mrs. Armstrong marching toward them, Julianna's smile vanished.

"It's not funny anymore," she whispered out of the side of her mouth to Jason. He saw what she saw and his smile disappeared too.

The director hurried over. "What happened?" she asked through clenched teeth, somehow implying that they might be making her look bad.

Jason and Julianna shrugged, wagging their heads simultaneously.

"Hers hit mine," Jason announced clumsily. Julianna winced at his lack of tact.

"Trevor seems to have tapped Amanda," she explained a little more smoothly, hoping somehow to save the service hours for both of them.

"Oh," Mrs. Armstrong said. She seemed relieved. "That type of behavior is actually quite age appropriate for this developmental stage," she began.

From there on Julianna was able to hear only fragments of sentences through the noise of the howling four-year-olds in her ears. She nodded respectfully, pretending to be enlightened by every word. Jason was squinting and nodding as well, obviously also unable to hear. Julianna almost laughed again.

". . . developmental, age appropriate, inappropriate, misplaced, repressed, latent, catalyst, and overt . . ." Mrs. Armstrong droned on.

Through the noise, Julianna was able to get the gist of this long-winded explanation even though she didn't buy it.

"So you see," the director said, her voice rising to deliver her final sentence, "it all is completely developmentally age appropriate."

She seemed completely satisfied with herself. She nodded at the four of them, Mary Poppins style, and said, "So I will leave the rest to the two of you."

With this she turned on her heel and strode away. Jason looked at Julianna in a panic as he realized that the director was leaving them in charge of the whole mess.

"Relax," Julianna said, glad Mrs. Armstrong was gone.

"Follow me," she told him, scooping up Trevor. "Get yours."

Dutifully, Jason picked up Amanda and followed

Julianna. She led him across the basement to a couple of empty chairs positioned against the wall.

"What did she say?" Jason asked, wide-eyed. Julianna sighed and over her shoulder she explained.

"She said he hit her because he likes her."

Jason screwed up his face. "Does that make sense?" he asked, flabbergasted.

"It doesn't to me," Julianna said. "But I'm not a four-year-old boy either."

"I am—uhh, I mean, was," Jason stuttered, suddenly self-conscious.

"Trust me," Julianna said. "You still are."

"Hey," he said in mock disgust.

Together they laughed.

Julianna plopped Trevor into one chair, and Jason put Amanda in the one next to him. The children continued to howl, noses high in the air, while Julianna snatched four candy canes off the nearby Christmas tree. She unwrapped them quickly.

"Do you have any idea what to do?" Jason asked.

"I know exactly what to do," she told him. And she did. She popped the first cane into Amanda's screeching mouth, the next into Trevor's, and a third into Jason's. Instantly, the three of them were silent, just as she knew they would be.

"Always works," she stated happily, popping the last

one into her own mouth. The two four-year-olds licked joyfully. Jason did the same.

Julianna didn't care what the manual said. Instinctively she knew what to do. She didn't have to think about it.

Julianna crouched before the two children while Jason stood behind her.

"You," she began, facing Trevor with just the correct combination of gentleness and sternness. Poking him playfully in the tummy, she said "You may not hit people."

"I not hit her," Trevor corrected between loud sucking noises. "Me punch her."

Julianna stifled a chuckle, amused by his innocent honesty. "I know," she acknowledged. "Why would you do that?"

"Me like her." He shrugged matter-of-factly, swinging his legs back and forth. Julianna's heart melted. He was hilarious. Behind her she heard Jason gasp in amazement.

"That's wild," he said as if he had just witnessed a miracle. "Just like the lady said."

Julianna found his amazement funny and was glad that he couldn't see her grinning. "And you," she continued, turning to face Amanda. She playfully poked Amanda's tummy. "You may not howl like a siren over almost nothing." Amanda giggled.

"You say 'I'm sorry,' " she instructed Trevor.

"Sorry," Trevor mumbled, examining exactly which stripes he had sucked off of the candy cane.

"And you say 'That's okay,' " she encouraged Amanda.

"That's okay," Amanda said, more than happy to comply.

"Now," Julianna said brightly, "let's be done with all of this nonsense and have some Christmas fun."

They skipped alongside her back to the craft table. She thought she heard Jason mutter "wow" again behind her.

The time passed easily with the common bond of the children uniting them. The teenagers laughed and chatted sometimes with Trevor and Amanda, sometimes with each other. Julianna learned that Jason had two sisters, wanted to be a lawyer like his father, and liked Cap'n Crunch cereal so much that he ate it out of a mixing bowl.

When he wasn't watching, Julianna studied his face, trying to imagine what it would be like for a boy like that to like her, to really like her.

They spent the remainder of the afternoon pleasantly, making cotton-ball snowmen, hand-print Christmas trees, and Popsicle-stick mangers. They sat in a circle on the carpet and sang Christmas carols and listened to Mrs. Armstrong read "'Twas the Night Before Christmas." Finally it was time to go.

Trevor's and Amanda's parents came at the same time. Together Julianna and Jason carried the giggling children to them. Julianna gave Trevor a kiss on the cheek. Jason gave Amanda a high five.

Alone, they stood self-consciously surrounded by the comings and goings of the others.

"Well, I guess that's it," Jason said.

"Yeah, I guess so," Julianna agreed.

"We got our hours," he offered.

"Yes, we got our hours," she repeated.

"It wasn't too bad," he said.

"No," she replied. She knew she was being sensitive, but she hoped he had enjoyed his time and not just thought it was not too bad.

"Well, I guess that's it," he said again, this time swinging his arms back and forth at his sides.

"Yeah. I guess so," Julianna agreed, her heart sinking a little deeper into her chest. They stepped away from each other at almost the same time.

"Bye," he said.

"Bye," she said.

"Merry Christmas," he offered.

"Merry Christmas," she said, feeling sad that it was all over. She tried not to stare at him as he walked away, but then she let herself, thinking why not.

She gathered her things, sliding on her coat, gloves, and scarf. All of a sudden she felt tired. It was as if she were a balloon, once flying high but now somehow the air had seeped out until she was flat on the ground.

She trudged up the basement steps and pushed the heavy metal door. It screeched open to reveal the bitter cold evening. The sky was dark and cloudy. When she looked up at the steeple light, she could see flurries of snow dancing around it. She walked along on the sidewalk cobblestones that went around the perimeter of the building. When she turned the last corner, she eyed the statue of Mary that sat tucked away in the bushes surrounded by dormant rose bushes. She realized that although she passed the statue several times a week, she almost never even really paused to look at it unless it was surrounded by the beautiful blooming summer roses. But today something drew her to it. The statue looked pretty even without the roses around it. Below the statue was a single small spotlight. The light was weak and flickering a bit, and the angle was wrong so that half of Mary's face was in the shadow and half was in the light. Julianna crouched down and found the bulb. She swept the dried leaves away and tightened the bulb so it stopped flickering. She used her scarf to polish the lens, then repositioned the light so that all of Mary's face was gently, beautifully illuminated. She made it perfect, then knelt to pray. She breathed deeply, letting the cool air come in and out of her. She decided on a simple "Hail Mary." When she was done she asked Mary to bless her and keep her and guide her. She was just about to get up when suddenly a bold punch landed on her arm. It almost knocked her over. She looked up and gasped. Ja-

son was standing above her with his gigantic proud smile. She clutched her arm.

"Why in the world would you pu—" Julianna stopped herself. She had been about to ask him why he had punched her. But she realized by his big goofy grin that she knew exactly why.

Still smiling, he said, "I'm not real sure why I punched you," he said teasingly. "You seem to be able to figure these things out."

He was absolutely the cutest thing she had ever seen.

"Okay," she said, grinning back at him.

"Okay," he said, appearing quite satisfied with himself. "See you at school," he said with a laugh.

"See you at school."

He stood there for another second, nervously shifting his weight from foot to foot.

"Well, Merry Christmas . . . again."

"Merry Christmas." Julianna blushed.

Peering from around the bushes until he was out of sight, she watched him walk away. Then, once he was gone, still kneeling, Julianna looked at the statue of Mary, studying Mary's face. The serene smile seemed to be saying that she understood. Before getting up, Julianna whispered "Thank you."

Her heart danced as she started for home and Christmas Eve dinner with her family.

ADRIANNA

She opened the closet door and eyed the half-used rolls of Christmas wrap. She decided on the blue foil with the silver snowflakes and a white satin bow. She took a roll of tape and a pair of scissors from the top shelf. On the floor in the hallway with just the glow of light from the rising sun, she carefully cut the paper to size. She looked at the gold ring, rubbing it with her thumb and forefinger to give it a slight shine. Then she placed it in the box and carefully wrapped it, folding and taping the edges. Then she placed the bow on top and she crept back into the bedroom. She set the box on the night table, taking care not to wake the sleeping figure in the bed. She held her breath when he sighed and rolled over. Within a moment he had settled. But she didn't let herself breathe again until she was out of the room.

A few minutes later she was driving down the highway. The wet Christmas Eve snowflakes smashed against the windshield then dripped down the glass as the tears of a broken heart dropped from her eyes and slid down her face. She went to the only place where she ever felt at home—the church. She drove into the deserted lot.

She pulled open the heavy wooden door and slid inside. The warmth surrounded her. She stomped the snow off of her furry winter boots. The stillness and quiet were deafening and made her question if she could hear at all. She looked around the empty church.

"I'm home," she whispered upward. Something her mother taught her. When she was a child, her mother would usher her and her sisters into the church, guide them to kneel and pray, and say, "Tell your Father you are home. The church is truly your home. As long as there is an open church door, you have a home."

Unable to pray at first, instead she just sat. She breathed deeply, trying to make it natural. She hadn't realized just how tense she had been or just how much she had been holding her breath. The church was cozy, and its warmth surrounded her like a hug. She did feel at home and safe within its walls, which was why for the first time in months she was actually able to cry. She let herself cry long and hard, just as children do. She just wished she was crying over something childish. But she wasn't. She was crying for a broken marriage, *her* broken marriage. Actually, part of what hurt so much was that it came as a bit of a surprise. Her marriage wasn't perfect, but she was happy and she thought her husband was too. But the fight the night before proved otherwise. She wrapped her arms around herself in a hug. An involuntary shiver wracked her. She sat in the pew reliving the events of the last evening. This time when she cried, it was like a grown-up, softly, with the tears gently falling down her face.

She thought back to the night before. The angry words raced through her head. Of course, it started over something small and stupid. Doesn't it always?

But at that moment for the life of her, she couldn't remember what. Was it because she commented that he had brought home fresh cranberries instead of the dried ones she had asked for? From there one snip led to a snap and it escalated, until they were practically—no, not practically—until they were screaming at each other. He called her rigid, suffocating, and unbending. She called him immature, unreliable, and undependable.

"Can't you ever do anything spontaneous?" he yelled.

"Well, give me a minute," she had screamed back. "I'll bake a cake and jump out of it for you."

Her eyes were wide with shock at her newfound courage. His eyes were angry as well.

"Anything's better than the way we live," he hollered. "Always planned by the book according to the to-do list," he sing-songed sarcastically.

It seemed that lately he was always criticizing her like that. She always stayed quiet, but not this time. This time the hurt was a little deeper and she asked him the question she had been afraid to ask him for years. "Well, why in the world did you marry me then?" And that's when he said it. He said the words she always feared to hear. The words that probably had kept her from speaking her mind all of those years. He said, "I don't know." The words stung her and took her breath away. She swore she wasn't able to breathe. And then there really was no place to go from there. On the inside she felt as if she had been kicked in the stomach, but on the outside her eyes stayed firm. This was another thing she had never done before—stayed firm. Her insides were shaking, but without even a hint of a quiver, she said, "Well, maybe we ought to do something about it then."

And without even a hint of hesitation he said, "Yeah, we should."

"Fine," she retorted.

"Fine," he agreed.

He stormed out, slamming the door behind him. She looked around the kitchen, wanting to slam a door back. Not finding one, she just stood frozen. She didn't let herself feel anything until she heard the garage door open then close again and she was sure he was gone. She was only able to stay mad for a while, then all of those feelings gave way to hurt.

She wandered around the house for the rest of the night. Her eyes dripped. There is no worse feeling than having someone you love be unhappy with you. It's surprising how easy it is to let someone go when you really love them. An odd paradox, she realized, but she knew she never wanted to see that look on his face again, the look that said he felt he was stuck with her.

Inside the church, she shuddered, bringing her back to the present, the evening before disappearing like a slow-moving fog. She held herself tight in a hug with her own arms wrapped around her and her warmest red sweater.

She dried her swollen eyes and sighed, then knelt and prayed. When she was done, she glanced around the church. A large wooden cross propped against the side wall caught her eye. It was the Cross of Christmas Blessings, a beautiful tradition in her church. People were encouraged to write their Christmas wishes on a small square of paper then nail it onto the cross. Then they were to take one of the squares already on the cross and pray for that person and their request throughout the Christmas season. It represented giving your problem to God, allowing Him to handle it. You were to give it with trust and faith. Then you were to carry someone else's cross by taking another's slip of paper, pray for them, and put yourself last. She got up and walked closer to the large cross. It was tilted up against a stained glass window. The deep rich colors of the glass were gently glowing. Scattered beneath the cross were a couple of tiny pencils and a few small squares of paper, and a miniature hammer and nails. The cross was bare. All the squares of paper had been taken. They had been written on with desperate hearts and taken by loving givers. All the prayers had been prayed. She was too late, she knew. Obviously it was too late for her to ask for a blessing. No one would be here to take it. But just the same, she knelt down and picked up one of the crumpled squares. She smoothed it out and scribbled her prayer, then took the hammer and a nail and carefully pounded it to the cross. Eyeing it, it looked sadly empty. She cocked her head sideways, kissed two fingers, then laid them on the slip of paper. Tears streaming down her face, she went back to the pew. Suddenly she was so tired. The sleepless night was catching up with her. She wrapped her arms more snugly around herself and drifted off to sleep, listening to the wind whistling through the church rafters.

Across town, he woke with a start. He darted up to a sitting position. He was in his own bed, but it still took him a few seconds to figure out where he was. Where would he be? He had woken up on this very side of this very bed for the last three years. He rubbed his eyes, remembering the night before. He checked the other side of the bed. She wasn't there. He leaned back, trying to see if she was in the bathroom. No light was on and the door was wide open. His head ached. He fell back onto the pillow and, when he did, his hand knocked into something on the night table. It was a gift, a Christmas gift. He sighed, relieved. She had forgiven him. He had spent half the night trying to figure out how he was going to apologize. In five years she had never made him apologize for anything, no matter how wrong he had been, so he had no idea how to. That's why it took him so long to come home. He rubbed the sleep out of his eyes and removed the bow, then ripped open the wrapping, smiling to himself in anticipation. The smile disappeared when he opened the box. He swallowed hard but somehow his throat was dry. He blinked. The ring was still there. He had no choice but to believe his eyes. His head swam. He jumped out of the bed and darted downstairs, calling her name, knowing full well that she wasn't going to answer. Knowing full well she wasn't there.

She woke up slowly, peacefully. She felt warm and safe. Her stomach wasn't in knots anymore. She remembered where she was. In the middle of the empty church she listened. It seemed as if the wind had calmed. She breathed in deeply. She looked over at the cross to see her folded prayer but stopped suddenly. She looked back at the cross and blinked. She distinctly remembered nailing her prayer to the right side of the cross. She scanned the church as she walked to the cross. The church was empty. She was sure she had nailed her prayer to the right side of the cross. But now it seemed to be on the left side. Deciding that she was mistaken, she wanted to make sure her prayer was still there.

At the cross, she stared at the paper. It looked like hers, but just to be sure, she pulled out the nail and unfolded the paper to find it wasn't hers at all. Instead it was a prayer that read "I want no one but you."

She swallowed hard. The handwriting was familiar. She turned, and instead of being startled by his sudden presence, she felt relieved. Her husband was standing in front of her, holding her paper prayer in his hand. Her prayer that said, "I wish that just once he would say that he wanted no one but me."

Their eyes met and misted with tears. Only a few words were necessary. They both smiled a weak smile that spoke the volumes only married people can speak without words.

He reached into his pocket and pulled out the present she had left him. He opened the box and removed her wedding ring. He smiled at her, big and boyish this time.

She blushed and smiled back. He got down on one knee and took her hand. She giggled.

"I want no one but you," he said.

And with just one tiny tear falling—a tear of joy this time—she simply said, "Okay." With that, he slipped the ring onto her finger. Then hand in hand, they walked to the church door. She looked back up at the altar and mouthed the words "Thank you." Once at the door, they looked out together at the snow that was now gently falling. She glanced down, noticing for the first time that he was still in his pajamas. She stifled a laugh.

"Oh," he said sheepishly, reaching into his coat pocket. "I think I got the right ones this time." He pulled out a plastic bag of exactly the right kind of dried cranberries. Adrianna only smiled and nodded.

"Let's make a run for it," he suggested. Holding hands with interlocked fingers, they ran across the parking lot as the snowflakes danced around them.

CASSANDRA

 "I need a minute," she said, trying unsuccessfully to force a smile onto her face that just wouldn't come.

As hard as she tried, she just couldn't seem to open her pursed lips.

"You okay?" he asked softly, avoiding eye contact to hide his own grim expression. He reached out and caressed the side of her face.

"Yeah," she said, willing her voice to sound perky. Instead it came out sounding more like a croak.

"Are these the ones?" he asked, holding up the bag of almonds she had asked for.

"They're great," she answered, barely audible. They stood in the hallway of their home, talking about everyday things like almonds, pretending that almonds mattered. Soon, thankfully, they were interrupted by the giggling and squealing of the two little girls who had just crashed into their legs and were now dancing and laughing in circles around them.

"I'm fine. Really," she said, this time her smile more convincing.

"I'll take them down to the car," he said. "Take your time. We're not due at your mother's for a while."

She watched as he took each little girl by the hand and led them down the stairs. They looked beautiful in their matching green and red velvet dresses, their hair done up in curls with Christmas ribbons and bows, their black patent leather shoes jingling with the bells that were clipped to them.

She turned and walked down the hallway, stopping when she got to the powder blue door. On tiptoes, she reached high and felt along the frame. Her fingers inched across until she found the key. She held it between her thumb and forefinger, feeling its cold smoothness. Her quivering hollow sigh was almost a shudder. Then she put the key in the lock and opened the door. "Merry Christmas, Doodle Bug," she called cheerily as she entered the room. The lump beneath the blue patchwork quilt wrestled within the bed. Then a messy-haired, blue-eyed, blond little boy popped his sleepy head out from under the covers.

"Hi, Mommy." He giggled. "I the baby bear," he announced proudly.

"I'm sorry. Hello, Baby Bear," she corrected herself. His smile broadened. She sat in the rocking chair and patted her lap invitingly. "Sit with me, Baby Bear."

"Okay, but just for a minute," he warned as he climbed onto her lap.

"Why just for a minute?" she asked.

" 'Cause in a minute I'm getting ready to be Superman."

"Oh, I understand," she replied.

" 'Cause I might be Batman too," he added.

"Of course," she agreed, smoothing his messy hair then mussing it again. "It's Christmas. What do you think of that?"

"It's pretty," he said.

"Do you like the lights?" she asked. "On the tree and outside?"

He nodded. "I saw them."

"Lots of snow."

"For Santa's sleigh," he reminded her.

"Will there be a present?" she asked in a teasing voice.

"A fire truck." He nodded surely. "There will be a fire truck."

"A red one?" she asked.

"A red one," he said firmly. "Like your sweater." He patted her sleeve gently. "I like red."

"Me too," she agreed.

"Hey," he said, his eyes widening. "Maybe there will be two presents!"

"I bet you're right," she said, giving his tummy a playful poke.

"Would you like me to read a story?" she asked.

" 'The Gingerbread Man!' " he yelled.

"Oh, not that one again." She groaned playfully.

"It's my favorite," he squealed indignantly.

"Oh, really?" His mother laughed. "I would never have known." She picked up the worn, tattered book and he nestled back into her lap.

She played with his toes as she animatedly read each word, stealing peeks at his beautiful face. His bright baby blue eyes, his round rosy cheeks, his long fluttering eyelashes.

Pure innocence. Pure beauty.

"I like that," he announced when she was finished reading. Then he darted off her lap and ran around circling the room shouting.

"Run, run as fast as you can. You can't catch me, I'm the Gingerbread Man!" She laughed and caught him as he returned to her, jumping on her lap.

"Do you know how much I love you?" she asked, tickling him. "Tell me, do you?"

"I do. I do." He laughed so hard he was unable to control his wiggling little body.

"Then tell me," she said, now kissing his tummy.

"Up to the sky," he squealed. "And down to China."

"You better believe it, baby. And Daddy loves you and so do Missy and Rachel," she reminded him.

"Daddy, Missy and Rachel, and you," he repeated carefully. "Hey," he said, turning to face her. He took her face in his two pudgy hands and looked deep into her eyes. "Am I still your baby?"

"Of course you are, silly," she said.

"But I three," he said in his gruff big-boy voice.

"I know, but you're still my baby forever."

"For big and little," he reminded.

"That's right. For big and little. For always."

"For always," he repeated.

"Let's look at your things," she suggested. She picked him up and carried him around the room in his fire truck pajamas examining the photographs on the walls.

"Here you are when you were born," she explained.

"I was a baby," he noted.

"A great baby," she clarified. "Soft and sweet and tiny.

"Here you are at the beach," she said.

"Big water," he commented.

"Big water," she repeated. "And here you are on Halloween."

"Hey, I'm a pumpkin!" he said, looking at her, confused.

"Everyone's a pumpkin on Halloween," she said. "Trust me. And here you are hunting for Easter eggs."

"Did I find any?"

"Oh yes, many," she assured him. "See, the basket is full." He nodded, satisfied.

"And here you are playing in the snow."

"What's that?"

"Your snowman, silly."

He laughed then yawned.

"I think my baby bear is getting tired," she murmured. He didn't protest.

"Should we pray?" she asked. He looked deep into her eyes and nodded. He snuggled into her lap and stayed very still as she recited the Our Father, the Hail Mary, and the Glory Be.

When she was done, she helped him make the sign of the cross with his hand, then kissed his pudgy fingers. Then she picked him up and hugged him tightly. His hair had the sweet smell of baby shampoo. She lay him in his bed, where he turned over and wiggled into position. She loved to watch him as he plugged his thumb into his mouth and prepared for sleep.

"I love you, my baby," she whispered.

He took his thumb out of his mouth to say, "I love you, my mommy."

She gulped back tears. "I love you much." She smiled softly, baiting him into a favorite exchange.

"I love you mucher," he exclaimed.

Then he stuck his thumb back in his mouth and settled again. She watched his eyes close.

In only moments his breathing became regular. He was sleeping peacefully. She covered him gently, took one long last look at his beautiful face, then sat down in the rocking chair and cried. When she was done, she looked heavenward and said, "Merry Christmas, Baby Bear. Mommy loves you . . . and misses you."

Then she got up and took one last look around the empty room.

She closed the door and locked it.

As she walked down the steps, she could hear the sounds of her daughters giggling.

She was grateful for the laughter. It was healing. Heavenward she whispered, "Thank you."

Then she wiped the tears off her face and practiced her smile.

VICTORIA

"Did you put out the nativity scene I gave you?" the voice on the other end of the phone asked.

"Of course I did," she said, flinching with guilt while mouthing the words "I'm sorry" heavenward, begging forgiveness for her little white lie. She had not put the nativity scene out but would, she swore to herself. She would put it out the second she got home.

"Does it look nice?" she asked.

"Beautiful!" she gushed. Her mother was killing her with these questions. She hadn't even unpacked it yet. The shame was suffocating her.

"Good," her mother said brightly. "Victoria?"

Here it comes, she thought. That tone in her mother's voice was undeniable. Her mother was about to lecture her about what was really important in life. She would tell her that the fact that Victoria was a doctor was absolutely wonderful. That she had chosen to follow in her father's footsteps was so touching. And the fact that she spent her days helping others in their time of need was, well, almost saintly—"but" she would tell her. It was the "but" that she really wanted to impress upon her. There's more to life than your work. You need to find someone to spend your life with. Victoria would protest that she was happy and fulfilled (a favorite word of her mother's). Her mother would insist that she would never know how happy she could be until her prince arrived. "Mom, please!" she would groan. "What am I supposed to do, go out on the highway and flag down cars? No, I know, I'll put an ad in the paper!" she offered in mock excitement. "Victoria," her mother would say with a sigh, "just promise me you'll try. Because you know you don't even try." They had been having these conversations for the last couple of years, and at first Victoria paid them no mind. But lately she had to admit she had been feeling a little lonely. Actually she had been feeling lonely for quite some time.

At first she truly just didn't know what she was feeling. But she found herself being interested in couples—just kind of watching them from afar. She watched how they interacted with one another and supported each other. She noticed that love took on so many more forms than she ever knew existed. Lately she found herself envious. Envy was not an emotion Victoria had felt often in her life. She was the smart sister, athletic enough and pretty too. Just about everything she ever wanted to do had come to her rather easily. She never had to work hard at much. She knew early on that she wanted to be a doctor, and although there was a lot of hard work involved, it was more of a matter of just doing it. Medicine had always been her love. Her work fulfilled her, and honestly, she never yearned for another type of fulfillment. She dated, but on her own terms. She could always find an escort for any formal function she needed to attend so the fact that she was not attached to anyone hadn't seemed to matter—until lately. It began like a dull gnawing in the middle of her stomach. She honestly didn't know what it was. It wasn't until she caught herself watching couples that she began to entertain the thought that just maybe there was something more. She watched her coworkers rush home to someone. Where once that looked like a hardship, lately it looked like it might be kind of nice to have someone to go home to and lean on. For the first time in her life Victoria felt like she couldn't just go out and instantly get what she wanted. She realized she didn't know the first thing about attracting a man. To be honest, the thought of trying to actively entice one embarrassed her.

"Are you hearing me?" her mother's voice rang through the cell phone. Her thoughts had drifted.

"I am, Mom," she promised.

"What about that new neighborhood of yours?" she asked. "I hear it's full of young people. Certainly everyone can't be attached."

Victoria had just bought a townhouse in a newer development. "Mom," she groaned. "What do you want me to do, hang out a sign, 'Desperate Unattached Girl Lives Here'?"

"Have a party," her mother offered promptly.

"And invite who?" she asked incredulously. "I don't know anyone!"

"What do you expect? Them to come knocking on your door?"

She wanted to say that that's the only way she was going to get to meet them, but she didn't. She knew her mother's heart was in the right place. There was no way she could admit to her mother how insecure she felt about dating. She could barely admit it to herself. Secretly, and maybe a little childishly, she wished her mother would guess. But after all these years of being the strong, overachieving daughter, it was unfair of her to expect her mother to read so deeply between the lines.

"Well, at least your nativity scene's out," her mother said. Victoria swore the woman had a sixth sense. She shook her head. She could probably see right through the phone.

"Why would it matter?" she asked.

"Because only good people put out nativities. It helps people weed people out."

"Mom, really." Victoria laughed.

"Don't laugh," her mother admonished. "It's true."

"Okay," she said, still laughing.

"What time will I see you? Do you need to sleep first?" her mother asked. "Were you busy last night?"

"Not too busy," Victoria said. "Things were pretty quiet. I got a little sleep. I'm just going to catch a few hours of sleep and then I'll be right over. I'd never miss Christmas Eve."

"That's my girl," her mother said. "Oh, you didn't forget the celery, did you?"

"No," Victoria said. "Got it right here."

"Good girl," her mother complimented her. "Love you, honey."

"Love you, Mom," she answered as she pulled her car into the driveway. Then she shut off the phone and the engine and sat in the car.

It was funny how she said she would never miss a Christmas Eve with such exuberance. If the truth be told, she couldn't remember the last time she felt Christmas. Year after year Christmas came and Christmas went, but she never really felt it. She guessed she meant Christmas spirit. What she really remembered, though, was that little tickling of excitement inside her tummy that she used to feel as a child. As a girl she felt it all of the time, of course. But as she grew she felt it less and less. Did anyone over twelve really feel true Christmas spirit?

She leaned back in the seat and looked up at the winter sky. It was full of puffy clouds that she wished would arrange themselves into the face of Jesus or a cross or even a Santa Claus or a Christmas tree, something to make her feel the hope and spirit of the season. As she looked up as if to say "I'm right here. Don't forget about me," she brushed something off her cheek. She screwed up her face, puzzled. It couldn't have been a tear because she hadn't cried since she was a kid.

She got out of the car. The harsh wind smacked her in the face. The sky was looking more ominous by the second. She better hurry. After unlocking the door, she charged into the apartment, only to almost trip over scattered moving boxes. She really needed to unpack. She should at least try to make the place look like a home. Her eyes darted from box to box as she tried to figure out which one held the nativity scene her mother had given her.

"Okay," she crooned when she spotted it, "let's get you guys out of there." She dragged the box out onto the balcony. One by one she pulled the pieces out, arranging them in the corner. It was a bit of a struggle, as the wind was picking up. Mary kept falling into Joseph. The Wise

Men toppled onto the little lamb, and the shepherd seemed determined to knock over the Baby Jesus. She all but slammed Joseph upright, then felt guilty. Once they were all in their places, she stared at them, smiling. "You're a good-looking group," she said softly. They looked beautiful. The purple-gray sky gave them a glow even without the bulbs being lighted. Right now they seemed to be lighted by the light above, God's light.

"Cool," she whispered, giving them one last look, then glancing up at the menacing sky. "Definitely looks like snow," she murmured, puzzled. Had snow been forecast?

Inside, she lay on the couch with the intention of just resting her eyes but instead fell asleep wondering if she'd ever find her Christmas spirit again.

An hour later she jumped, startled, out of a sound sleep. She had been so deeply asleep that at first she didn't even know where she was or what had woken her. During all of those nights of sleeping on call at the hospital, it was always the screech of her pager that awoke her, but not this time. Confused, she looked around. A loud rapping came from the front door. She couldn't imagine who it could be. She didn't know anyone. It was probably someone trying to leave a package for one of her neighbors.

Grudgingly, she went downstairs. When she opened

the door, she was nearly blinded by the bright light. Her eyes grew wide. What in the world had happened while she had slept? It must have snowed a foot. Blocking almost the entire doorway was the most humongous sheepdog she had ever seen. Squinting into the glare, she could make out the silhouette of a woman who was struggling to hold the dog back.

"Sorry," she said, huffing and struggling. "Whalen, pleeease!"

"Sorry," she said to Victoria again. "Hey, Merry Christmas," she managed. "Is this camel yours?" Then the woman realized that she hadn't produced a camel. "Oh, wait," she said with an embarrassed laugh as she struggled with the dog's leash, which was fast becoming tangled around her. With a groan she yanked a plastic camel out of her coat.

"Here, this one."

This time they laughed together.

"Yes, he's mine," Victoria said, recognizing the plastic figure from her nativity scene. "I guess that storm was pretty bad." She used her hand as a visor to shield her eyes so that she could see better. It helped the neighbor to come into focus.

"I'm Page from down the street," the woman explained. "And this is Whalen." She all but groaned. "Lovable but out of his mind."

Victoria laughed. "Sometimes the best combination."

Victoria noticed Page was a pretty, middle-aged woman with salt-and-pepper, perfectly coiffed hair. Something about Page's face made her seem familiar. Her eyes? Her nose? Her freckles? Victoria couldn't decide. Page wore tight-fitting running clothes beneath an extra-large sweatshirt and coat. The sweatshirt read "I do it," and Victoria decided she did. Page didn't look like one of those people who wore exercise clothes as a fashion statement; she really worked out in them. Her slim figure was testimony to that. Suddenly Victoria felt out of shape— maybe a New Year's resolution? she thought, making a mental note.

"That was quite a snow, wasn't it?" Page said.

"I guess so," Victoria agreed, still feeling as if she were Rip Van Winkle and had woken up out of a forty-year sleep.

"I like your nativity," Page said. "I noticed it this morning, before the storm."

"Thanks." She liked Page already. "A gift from my mom."

"Neat," said Page, her eyes twinkling. "Well, welcome to the neighborhood," she added, holding tightly to Whalen, who seemed determined to get into the house. "I'm in 301. Knock anytime. Maybe we could walk together."

"Okay," Victoria answered quickly, meaning it. "I

will. Hey, thanks," she added, holding up the camel. "And Merry Christmas."

After she closed the door, a face of a childhood friend flashed into Victoria's mind. Page looked familiar because she had the same freckles and eyes of Victoria's first-grade friend Jenny. On her way up the stairs, Victoria smiled, thinking that sometimes God is playful.

She went out to the balcony door to replace the camel. She blinked, not believing her eyes. Except for the manger, the entire nativity scene was gone, every single piece. The space where it had sat was covered with a pile of newfallen snow. She looked down over the balcony rail, but for as far as she could see, there was only a blanket of undisturbed white. Where in the world had they all gone?

From out on the balcony she could hear the faint sound of her doorbell ringing again. "It doesn't ring once in four months," she muttered to herself on her way down the stairs, "now it's ringing every two minutes." This time when she opened the door, standing before her were two older women who looked to be in their seventies.

"Helloooooooo," they yodeled in unison before Victoria had a chance to open her mouth. They were dressed identically in matching blue wool caps, red mittens, and purple parkas. They were fit and lively. An identical thick patch of bangs stuck out from under their caps. Once she had a chance to take a longer look at them, she could tell that they had identical faces. Up close their energy was almost overwhelming.

"I'm Addie," said one.

"I'm Maddie," piped the other.

"Actually," they said together.

"Adeline," one clarified.

"And Madeline," the other followed.

"We're sisters. And twins."

These last two announcements were made in unison; it sounded like one voice. They spoke with such great exuberance it wasn't hard to realize just how proud they were of each other and of themselves.

"It's nice to meet you." Victoria laughed.

"Oh, it's nice to met yooou!" they insisted so boisterously she knew that these two refused to be outdone.

"We were out for a stroll," the one began.

"And the strangest thing happened," the other continued.

"We stumbled across these Wise Men!"

"Imagine!" one of them began. "Two wise women stumbling over three Wise Men," they exclaimed together, then laughed, almost screeching. Then without warning their collective expression turned on a dime.

"We really stumbled!" the one explained, nodding seriously. "If they are yours, you really should be more responsible with your things, dear."

A bit taken aback by the impromptu scolding, Victoria opened her mouth to apologize but found the moment gone before she could catch it. These ladies moved fast.

"Poor things," they both said now, shaking their heads side to side and staring at the Wise Men as if they were real.

Wanting somehow to grab onto this situation, Victoria clumsily jumped in. "Yes, they are my Wise Men," she blurted. "And I am so, so sorry you stumbled on them." She was talking quickly because she was afraid she might not get another chance. "But I do thank you for returning them."

"Returning them *safely*," one added.

"We're returning them safely," the other insisted.

"Yes, yes you are," Victoria agreed. She was beginning to find the humor in the situation and swallowed a laugh. "And I really do thank you both," she repeated, enunciating each syllable. These ladies obviously needed thanking more than once to feel appropriately appreciated.

"I'll be sure to put them right back," Victoria assured.

Thankfully, the sisters seemed to be a little short on focus on other things and turned their attention back to themselves, where Victoria suspected it was most of the time anyway.

"Remarkable," one hissed.

"Yes, remarkable," the other one agreed, seeming to know exactly what her sister was referring to.

"Yes. We really are remarkable showing up like this, just in the knick of time!"

"Oh, yes!" Victoria agreed, relieved that they were pleasant again. She realized these ladies loved to find themselves in the middle of coincidences, coincidences that were real or created. And she also guessed that they were very often the heroines in these episodes.

"Well, tootle loooh!" one yodeled.

"Yes, tootle loooh!" the other echoed.

As she closed the door, Victoria decided they were lovely but exhausting. This time she climbed the steps slowly, laughing to herself. She decided she liked those ladies. She might run the other way when she saw them, but she liked them. Then she went out to the balcony, re-placed the three Wise Men, and took a long look at the lonely pieces. The absence of the others gave her just the slightest pang of sadness. She hoped they'd come back.

She went inside to put on a pot of tea. She guessed that her nap was over. As she waited for the water to boil, she daydreamed. An odd tapping drew her from her thoughts. She wasn't sure what she was hearing. It started off faint, then grew a little louder. It was an odd sound.

Sort of like a tap, followed by a trickle. She emerged from the kitchen and stood in various locations in the apartment, listening. She was in the bedroom when she finally heard it again. She darted into the living room, trying to catch the sound. It definitely came from there. She waited and waited and then it happened again. Her eyes widened when she realized that someone was throwing snowballs at the balcony door. "Who in the world would do something like that?" she asked herself, exasperated. After she threw open the glass door, she quickly discovered just who would do something like that. Standing below the balcony was a teenage girl. Actually to say simply that she was a teenager did not begin to do her justice. If the truth be told, she was the most splendid example of "teenager" that Victoria had seen in quite a while. She was dressed like she had just come out of a catalog, with matching white-fur-trimmed hat, gloves, and boots. Her jacket was a baby pink and tiny. It stopped short of covering her exposed tummy. Her belly button was pierced. Victoria thought she saw a snowflake ring, but she couldn't be sure.

She had a good mind to ask what kind of person throws snowballs at a door like that, but she reminded herself that the girl was a child and it was Christmas.

"Hi," Victoria called down to her.

"Hi," the girl chirped back. "Is this Mary like yours?" She was holding the plastic Mary from the nativity scene.

"Yes, she's mine," Victoria said. She got almost the first syllable of thank-you out, but it was missed because the girl was off and running.

"Oh, good!" she said dramatically, as if to suggest that they had both just avoided tragedy. But then she sped off. "So like I was coming home from Diaaaaana's houuuuuuuuuse. We just had a fight, agaiiiiiiiiiiiiin. Like our eightieth this week." Her head bobbed wildly up and down as she spoke. "She's been like hanging out with Nina and Marissa when I was at the orthodontist and she's like 'no I wasn't' and I'm like 'yes you were' and she's like 'no I wasn't' and I'm like 'yes you were.' So we had a fight," she stated firmly, her head bobbing. This last sentence was punctuated with eye rolling. "And I'm sure I will never, like, speak to her again. So anyway, I was hurrying 'cause I guess when you're mad you hurry or something and I looked down and like there it was. And I'm like, what is that? Then I'm like, oh my gawwwwd. It's like Mary. Like Mary, Mary." She took a big gulp of air, which Victoria was sure she needed because her entire monologue had come out in a huge rush.

"I'm Natalie, by the way," she said. She had an amazing way of speaking. She was completely animated and completely enjoyable to watch. She began each sentence very quickly then suddenly screeched to a halt, sped off again, then finally ended by drawling out the last two words while raising her voice, making every sentence sound like a question. Each sentence was peppered with "like," "you know," gum snapping, and eye rolling.

It took Victoria a moment to realize that the girl was finished.

"Oh, yes." She blinked "It was Mary, Mary," she confirmed, then laughed out loud, realizing how dumb her statement must have sounded. She knew the girl would not notice her laughing.

"And thanks a lot for returning her," she added. She thought the conversation might be over, but she realized otherwise when the girl continued to stand in front of her, half nodding, half bobbing her head up and down. She seemed to be waiting for something more. Suddenly she seemed so young. All dressed up but still a little girl. Victoria realized that she was waiting to be talked to.

"So," she began awkwardly ignoring the freezing temperature. "Where do you live?"

"Oh, in the neighborhood," Natalie answered, waving her arms wildly in opposite directions.

Victoria nodded. Natalie was cute.

"With your mom and your dad?" Victoria realized that she had no idea how to talk to a teenager.

"Oh, yeahhhhhhh," she oozed in the singsong manner Victoria liked. "Yeah, with both of them." The words rushed out. "I mean, they're not divorced or anything. I mean, I don't know why." She shrugged, furrowing her brow. "Everyone is."

Victoria stifled a laugh, deciding that Natalie came from a happy home. "Well, good for them," she said with a touch of sarcasm. "Do your relatives come for the holiday?"

"Naaaaaaaahhh," Natalie replied. "They're all old and afraid to drive in the snow. Which is completely lame if you ask me 'cause when I get my license, I'm gonna drive in anything. I won't care."

"I bet you won't," Victoria agreed.

"Hey, do you got a kid? I babysit," Natalie announced suddenly, switching directions. Victoria realized that a person had to pay attention when talking to Natalie. She found it strange that Natalie thought she might be someone's mother. She just never thought of herself as looking the part.

"Well, actually, I *will* babysit," Natalie corrected. "I will babysit after I take my CPR class at the Y. So if you got a kid, call me."

Victoria started to explain that she wasn't a mother, but Natalie didn't leave any room for her to nudge a word in.

"Call me, not Diana, 'cause I like her, you know. But I'm way more responsible. Her fish keep dying and she left her glasses at the pool three times last summer. Her mother freaked. I mean, about the glasses. Her mother was kind of sick of the fish."

Victoria wasn't sure she could keep a straight face

much longer. She was finding this hilarious. "Well, you be sure to stop by sometime, Natalie," she said, reaching down to take hold of the Mary figure.

"Can I bring Diana?" she asked quickly. "And maybe Nina and Marissa?"

"Of course." Victoria laughed. "I would love to meet them."

"Yeah, but remember what I told you." Natalie shook her head solemnly.

"Oh, for sure," Victoria promised, letting herself laugh out loud. "See you."

"See you," Natalie said.

Victoria watched as the girl hopped across the backyard, carefully retracing her steps by jumping into the tracks she had made on her arrival.

"Welcome back, Mary, Mary," Victoria said, looking the figure in the eyes. Gently she replaced her in her original spot, wondering what had become of the others.

Back inside, Victoria sat with her cup of tea and stared out the balcony door at the bright white snow. She decided that no human could ever duplicate the pure white that God could create.

Then the doorbell rang, cutting into her thoughts. Instead of startling her this time, it felt familiar, almost friendly. She laughed out loud as she hopped downstairs to answer it. Open to the idea of whoever it might be.

At the door was a large, burly man. It took only a

minute for Victoria to realize that God had blessed him with a voice to match his physique.

"Hello," he all but yelled. "Merry Christmas. I'm Ed from down the street. Is Joseph yours?"

Victoria had been so intent on his huge figure and booming voice that she hadn't noticed the plastic figure he had tucked under his arm. It was the Joseph from her nativity scene.

"I guess he was looking for a place to stay. You didn't by chance have told him 'no room at the inn,' did ya?" He laughed so long and heartily at his own joke that it was impossible not to laugh with him. He seemed almost completely unaware that up until now he was the only one who had said anything. He seemed more than comfortable carrying on both sides of the conversation.

"Yes, he's mine," Victoria said. "Thanks."

After a few more pleasantries, Ed proclaimed himself the go-to man. "If you need it moved or lifted, I'm your guy," he explained. "Just call me. All the ladies do." He beamed proudly. "My wife says it's the least I can do. She says I gotta put all this," he exclaimed, waving his arms, "to good use."

"Well, thanks," Victoria said, taking Joseph from him.

"You be sure to call," Ed said. "Pretty thing like you shouldn't be moving her own stuff."

"I will," Victoria promised. She decided Ed was one

of those truly nice guys. He turned to go, then stopped and jumped as if he had almost tripped over something.

"Ooops!" he bellowed. "Well, hello there, you two! Merry Christmas. Have a good day now." When Ed moved out of the way, Victoria was surprised to find an elderly couple standing before her. She blinked, startled to see them. Ed's large frame had completely eclipsed them. How long had they been waiting patiently behind him?

"Excuse us," the man said, speaking for the both of them.

They were quite small and, if Victoria were to say in the most respectful way, amazingly cute. They were bundled well for the weather and hunched over at what seemed to be the exact same angle.

They stood perfectly silent for a moment.

"It is very nice to meet you," the man said in almost a whisper. He bowed slightly at the waist as he introduced them. "This is Angeline," he said, nodding to his wife. "And I would be Frank." The old woman nodded her head eagerly in agreement with a bright, beautiful smile on her face. Frank obviously was the spokesman for the two. She didn't seem to mind.

"Oh, it's nice to meet both of you," Victoria said, hoping that she didn't sound condescending. They were just so adorable.

As she herself aged, she found herself almost in awe

of the elderly. Especially older married couples. There was something so beautiful about them. She admired the commitment they had made and the history they kept on making, and these two standing before her obviously possessed all of this and more. She noticed they were holding hands and her heart melted.

"We are very happy to welcome you to our neighborhood," he said kindly, and she knew he was genuine. She detected a touch of an accent, but she wasn't sure from where.

"Thank you," she said. "I like the place."

"Us, too." He smiled. "Been good."

Victoria nodded.

"If you need us," he said, "we are number 308."

"Oh, thank you," Victoria said. "And if you ever need me, I'm right here." She decided they were going to be her favorite neighbors.

"Now business," he announced with a playful smile on his face. "The lambs. Maybe yours?" They each held up one plastic lamb from the nativity scene.

"Oh," Victoria said, "yes, they are. Thank you. I feel bad you carried them all this way."

"Is no problem," he assured her. Victoria thought she might have heard the old lady repeat "no problem" after him.

"We walk every day," he explained. "Every day for

fifty years." He nodded. "Rain, snow, big heat, whatever. So no problem."

"On our steps." The little woman giggled, holding a mittened hand up to her mouth. Her eyes were simply sparkling. Victoria suspected that she was quite the character. Her husband looked down at her with such love, it filled Victoria's heart with joy.

"Yes. We found them on our steps. What a surprise. Christmas and we find lambs." He laughed with her now.

The three of them laughed together.

"Well, I must take my little lamb home," the man announced. "She's getting cold, I know." He looked at her adoringly, and she looked back at him enjoying being adored.

"We see you. Merry Christmas," he said, waving his gloved hand.

Victoria leaned against the door frame and watched as they strolled back down the walk and down the street, holding hands. Their feet made tracks in the snow. Two by two. Side by side. Just the way they've gone through life, she thought. She went back into the apartment wondering if that would ever happen to her.

She reached the top of the stairs just in time to catch a glimpse of something out the balcony door. Whatever it was, it was fleeting. She stared, hoping to catch it again. After a moment she did. It was a head popping up, then down, then up again just above the edge of her balcony. Someone was jumping. Confused, she went outside, set the lambs in place, then peered over the side. Looking back at her was a man dressed in oxford shoes and blue trousers, with a golf sweater peeking out beneath a camel winter coat. He was of average build with sandy hair, somewhere in his forties.

"Hi," Victoria said.

Instead of waving or even smiling when he saw her, he tossed his head in kind of an upward, too-macho nod. It reminded her of high school. It practically said "I'm acknowledging you but still way too cool to say hello."

"Hi," Victoria said, this time forcing the smile.

"Hood. Steven Hood," he announced, more like he was "Bond. James Bond." She wanted to laugh and say "Tenley. Victoria Tenley." and upward nod him right back, but instead she just settled for "I'm Victoria."

"Four-seventeen Bayberry," he shot back. It took her a second to realize that he was telling her his address.

"Oh! Um, well"—she laughed—"I live right here." When there was no response, Victoria decided she wanted to move the conversation along. "So?" she said, palms up.

"Oh, here. Is this priest yours?" he asked, taking a plastic shepherd from under his arm. He jumped up and was able to place it into her hands. Now she understood what all his jumping before had been about. She wanted to laugh. At least he recognized it as something religious.

"Yes," she said. "He's the shepherd from my nativity scene."

"Oh." A slightly confused look crossed his face. It was there for only a second, then he shrugged it off.

"I'm in insurance," he said, jumping again and offering his hand. Victoria grazed it for the second it was there. Back on the ground, he said "Can't have too much" almost gravely while shaking his head.

"No, I guess not," she lied. Actually, Victoria thought you *could* have too much insurance.

"Got any?" he asked so abruptly that for a second she wasn't sure what he was talking about.

"Insurance? Oh, yeah, I've got some."

"Home?"

"Yes."

"Life?"

"Yes."

"Auto?"

"Yes."

"Health?"

"Yes."

If she ever came up from under this attack, she was going to laugh.

"Disability?!" He said this way too loudly, thinking he just might get her on this one.

"Yes," she said, laughing. "I have disability insurance."

"How much?" he fired at her.

Taken off guard, Victoria opened her mouth to speak but wasn't fast enough.

"See," he all but yelled. "Did you know," he said, his voice becoming hysterically dark, "most people don't have enough. Do you know that you could probably afford to die but not to become disabled?"

It took every bit of self-control Victoria possessed not to laugh out loud. What in the world did that mean?

"Mmmmmm" was all she could trust herself to mutter without breaking into laughter.

"I bet your husband could afford to die but not to become disabled!" He nodded surely.

Feeling bad for the poor underinsured husband she didn't have, she shrugged. As quirky as this guy was, Victoria decided there was good in him and she liked him.

"Your husband home?" he asked, trying to see around her frame, which was blocking the doorway.

"He's sleeping" she lied, amused.

"Okay, okay." He retreated. She was amused at the fact that he thought that he would be going to a higher power if he were to speak to her imaginary husband.

"Fire?" he shot at her suddenly.

"Yes."

"Flood?"

She paused. "No," she said, letting him win.

"Hah!" he hollered. "Got you!" Victoria was afraid he was going to break into some kind of end zone dance. "Don't feel bad," he consoled. "I get everyone on that one. Nobody thinks they need flood insurance until they do."

"Yeah, I guess so," Victoria conceded. She didn't want to ruin this victory for him, considering how much he was enjoying it. But she did remember specifically reading somewhere in the dozens of mortgage papers that there had never been a flood in the community, ever.

"So when are we going to take care of this?" he asked.

For a second Victoria had no idea what he meant. Then she realized that he wanted to sell her some flood insurance.

"O-oh," she stammered. "Soon, for sure. Right after the holiday."

"Great!" he yelled. Then he became solemn. "Hey, we're neighbors," he pointed out, as if to suggest this somehow made them family.

"I swear," he said with his hand on his heart. This must be the dramatic closing, she thought. "I swear. I won't sleep until we do."

"Oh, you are so kind," she said, sure he was too far gone to get any sort of sarcasm. "As soon as the holidays are over," she promised. "Really." She meant it. It couldn't cost much anyway.

Elated, he looked like a little boy. "Here, take my card," he said, jumping up to hand her one from the stack of about fifty he pulled from his coat like a magician. Then thinking better, he jumped again and handed her the entire stack. "For your friends," he explained.

"Thanks," she said, smiling and taking them. "Thanks again for my shepherd." One last time that confused look crossed his face as if to say "Are you sure that's not a priest?"

"Merry Christmas," she said.

"Oh, yeah," he said, turning back. "Yeah. Merry Christmas."

She laughed.

She replaced the shepherd and surveyed the group. They were all back but the Baby Jesus. The whole scene looked wrong without him. It made her sad. She wanted him back.

She went back into the house and sat quietly for a few moments partly enjoying the quiet, partly wishing the doorbell would ring. When it didn't, she went into the kitchen and cleaned and chopped the celery. She seasoned and stirred it, then put it into a container in the refrigerator to keep until she went to her mother's. After that she took a long hot shower and dressed in black slacks and the bright red sweater that she wore only once a year, on Christmas Eve.

Deciding it was time to head over to her mother's, she went to pull the shades on the balcony door. Looking out onto the nativity figures in the snow, she decided to straighten them one last time. She repositioned them, leaving just enough room for the missing Baby Jesus.

"Hey," said a voice from behind her. She turned to discover the most gorgeous pair of blue eyes looking back at her from the adjoining balcony.

"Hi" was all she could manage. Why was she flustered? She *never* got flustered. The eyes were attached to a six-foot-something black-haired guy about her age. With only inches between the balconies, she felt suddenly too close and took a step back. He smiled at her.

"Looks like I have something of yours," he said. She was so busy memorizing his face that she didn't notice he was holding her Baby Jesus figure in his hands. Only when he held it up, blocking his face, did she see it.

"Oh!" she exclaimed, coming out of her trance. Why was she acting so stupid?

"Oh, oh-oh," she added. Very intelligent, she thought. He laughed again, revealing the whitest teeth on the planet.

"None of it means much without him," he added, handing the figure to her.

"No, it doesn't," she said, becoming herself again.

"Thanks for putting it up," he said, motioning to the scene. "I can see it from my place. It's beautiful."

"Thanks. A gift from my mother," she added proudly.

"My mom sent me one for under my tree," he said.

"That's nice," she said with a grin. Her mother's voice saying "only good people put nativity scenes out" rang in her ears.

There was a small pause, but neither one of them wanted the conversation to end so they jumped in for more. He was staring into her eyes now.

"She sent me a small tree too—my mom did." He laughed, realizing that it sounded so awkward.

She laughed too. It was funny how they were squirming for small talk.

"Hey, I'm Peter, by the way." He offered his hand. She took it and for just a moment her hand melted comfortably into his. Victoria had to look away. She was sure her face would give her feelings away.

"Does she live close by?" she said quickly, taking her turn to pump life into the conversation.

"Nah." He shrugged with a hint of genuine disappointment in his voice. "My family is all out of town, and I've got to work for the holiday." For the first time she had the nerve to look up and look at all of him, and when she did she realized he was wearing medical scrubs. She almost laughed out loud, realizing that he was a doctor. Again she heard her mother's voice saying "There's someone out there for you, like you."

"How about you?" he asked.

"I'm lucky," she said, meaning it. "I'm on my way to my mother's now for dinner."

"Oh." They were looking at each other now.

"I guess I better go," she said.

"Okay." He shrugged. "Well, here he is," he said, gently handing over the Baby Jesus. She carefully took him from his hands. Their fingers touched slightly and she liked it.

"Hey," she said, reaching down for the plug. "Let me light it for you. This way you can see it from your place."

"Okay." He smiled.

And then she said it. And as soon as she did, she couldn't believe that she had. "I'll be back around ten. Do you want to come over for some hot chocolate or something?" Her stomach clenched as she saw him begin to shake his head "no" almost as the words left her mouth.

"I think we're supposed to drink eggnog." He laughed playfully.

Her face colored and she laughed in relief. "Okay, then we'll make it eggnog."

"Good," he said. "I'll feel a lot better about it that way."

He was gorgeous. She smiled at him. Then she turned and ever so gently laid the Baby Jesus in the manger. For a moment they looked at the beautiful scene together. The connection between them warmed her.

"Well," she said, wishing that the moment could last, "I guess I'll see you at ten."

"I'll be there," he replied. "Be careful," he added.

She blinked, startled. The words had sounded completely natural from him. "I will," she answered.

Just then a gentle breeze blew over them, sprinkling a mist of snowflakes. It made them both smile. Squinting, they looked upward and paused.

"Look at that cloud." He chuckled. "It looks like a reindeer."

She closed her eyes and smiled upward and thought "Close enough." When she looked, she could hardly believe it. It really *did* look like a reindeer. She saw it too. She gulped, her eyes misting a bit. Her tummy felt tickly.

Daring one last look at him, she said, "See you at ten."

"See you at ten," he repeated.

Victoria was halfway to her mother's house before she realized that the feeling inside her tummy was her long-lost Christmas spirit.

ALEXANDRA

Alexandra peeled back the corner of the curtain, peering with one eye out the window at the mailman disappearing down the sidewalk. He was later today than usual—only four minutes, but still later. She sighed, thinking herself pathetic. Who in the world knows when the mailman is four minutes late? "You do," she muttered, answering her own silent question out loud.

She took a deep breath, her stomach tied in expectant knots. She opened the door to the harsh December wind. Ice crystals rushed in, swirling around the entry. She turned her face sideways, trying to escape the splash, and felt blindly into the metal box to gather the mail. After she grabbed it, the lid clanged shut and she closed the door with a thud. She shivered and sat down on the staircase.

She hesitated, closing her eyes, wishing for just one small sign of hope. The Christmas Eve mail that she held in her hand was her last chance for hope until after Christmas, and she needed so badly to feel hope for Christmas. And the way she saw it, her only chance for hope would come in that day's mail or not at all.

She made herself look. Slowly she began to riffle through the stack of envelopes. One at a time she tossed them onto the marble floor as her heart and hopes sank. Then she stood up, turned and walked up the steps as the tears streamed down her face.

Sniffing, she entered the darkened bedroom. She leaned against the wall, her shoulders heaving. Then she slid down and sat with her knees tucked to her chest. After a while, all cried out, she sat calmly with her chin on her knees. She reached over to the wicker trunk beside her and opened the lid. Then she gently pulled out a tattered gray sweater.

She held it on her lap, carefully touching each of the pearl buttons. Closing her eyes, she pressed it to her face.

"Oh, Nunnie." She sighed. "Please be with me. I just needed to hear from you," she explained. Still clutching the sweater, she relaxed into a lazy daydream. She remembered all the times that her grandmother had been there for her. Her happy childhood was speckled with pleasant memories of her sweet words, loving touches, gentle laughs. Her face darkened as she remembered her untimely, sad death. But she knew her grandmother was still with her. She recalled the times throughout the years that she felt her grandmother's presence, the times when like a heaven-sent feather she had thrown down a comforting whisper. It had always felt like a gentle comforting kiss had been planted softly on her cheek, a kiss from her beloved grandmother. That she was the favorite was not spoken aloud, of course. But Alexandra and her sisters had known. Her grandmother was a wonderful woman who truly loved each of her granddaughters dearly, loving each for her uniqueness. She found the very best in each of them. It just happened that Alexandra was the granddaughter most like her, with qualities and interests that made them kindred spirits.

Her grandmother had tried to teach all of them the dying art of crocheting. With bundles of multicolored yarn and dozens of hooks, they sat before her in a semicircle around her rocking chair, chatting and giggling about glorious items they were surely going to crochet. Forty minutes later the only one left at her grandmother's knee was Alexandra, determined to manipulate the yarn and the crochet hooks, the others finding it too hard or boring when it didn't come to them instantly. So to this day it was Alexandra who everyone in the family calls when a new baby arrives and a blanket is needed. More than proficient now, Alexandra was happy to oblige. One year for Christmas her grandmother had given them each a small poinsettia plant. Trying to impart her love of gardening to her granddaughters, she said, "There will be something special for the one who brings it back alive at Easter dinner." All of them were sure they would be the one. "How difficult could it be to keep a silly old plant alive for just a few months?" "What's a little sun and water?" "Heck, to get the prize I'll even talk to it." Three months later only Alexandra had a blooming poinsettia to grace the table. And it was only Alexandra who walked out with the golden locket that her grandmother had awarded her.

When her grandmother had passed away, each of the granddaughters shed genuine tears, but Alexandra's came from a deeper place. All grown up by then, her sisters understood and respected this. When it was time to decide who would inherit their grandmother's house, they unanimously agreed that it should be Alexandra. Each gave her just one penny, with Alexandra giving them a quarter in change. This was a favorite game of their grandmother's. As children, whenever they wanted something from the corner candy store, they would say, "Grandma, I need more money." She would reply, "Nothing in this world is free. But sometimes a girl gets a bargain. Give me a penny and I'll give you a quarter." And she would. And off they would go to the candy store to collect their treats, with their grandmother laughing behind them. Later they would marvel at how none of them ever noticed that there might be something amiss in these transactions. Alexandra also was the only sister who inherited her grandmother's love for baking. It was Alexandra who took the time to sort through her grandmother's recipe box, experimenting with each cookie, cake, or pie again and again until she had re-created her grandmother's masterpieces. Alexandra would surprise them, showing up at holidays with something from long ago, something that brought back the flood of memories of sweet childhood times. In Alexandra, her grandmother was alive. Right down to her green-flecked eyes. Each sister had been blessed with a different combination of greens and blues, but only Alexandra's contained the flecks of gold that her grandmother's had.

And when her grandmother passed away, she had left them all—all except Alexandra, because in small ways her grandmother had stayed with Alexandra. Alexandra had made her grandmother's home her home. And inside it she felt her presence. She felt her presence in the usual ways that people tend to feel the presence of lost loved ones—in a blooming flower, a colorful sky, a fresh-fallen snow, a church hymn. Alexandra "heard" from her grandmother in all of these ways, but she also seemed to hear from her in a unique way. Not often—only when she seemed to really need to, at times when all hope seemed to vanish, when no one else's comfort could ever help—she would get mail from her grandmother. Just when she was sure that whatever life situation she was struggling with was not going to work out, she would reach into that old tin mailbox (she never dared change it from her grandmother's original) and pull out hope, a piece of mail addressed to her grandmother, a sign telling her that everything would be okay. And no matter what the situation, when she got the letter it never failed her. Whatever the problem was, it worked itself out somehow.

When she first moved into her grandmother's house, of course there was loads of mail for her. And of course Alexandra thought nothing of it. But after about a year, as the normal progression would have it, the letters all but stopped. Then for the next couple of years maybe one or two letters slipped by. By the fifth year, she got nothing.

She never gave it a thought. She never made the connection between mail for Nunnie and comfort when she seemed to need it most until it happened when she applied to graduate school. She so desperately wanted to get in. On the last day of the selection process, having received no letter or call from the university, she had lost hope. In that day's mail was a letter for her grandmother. Although she enjoyed seeing her name and thought it strange, it wasn't until the next morning, when the registrar's office called inviting her to register for classes, that she put the two together. She said a prayer of thanks to her. The next time was a year later, when she was struggling with her fiancé's horrendous betrayal and their breakup. Again she received mail for—or as she always saw it, mail *from*—her grandmother telling her that there would be another greater, more worthy love, and there was. A week later the man who was now her husband presented himself at a church dance. No more mail came, and she hadn't needed any until two years later, when she was struggling with infertility. The more they tried to get pregnant, the more anxious she became. Then one day out of a clear blue sky came mail from her grandmother. It touched her instantly, calming her. She knew exactly what it meant, and it helped her to put her worry exactly where it should be, exactly where it should have been all the while: in God's hands. Eleven months later she became a mother to the love of her life, her son, John. That was the last time.

But she had never wanted and needed mail from her grandmother more than this week. She pressed her swollen eyes to the tattered sweater one more time, then stood up. Then she stood directly in front of the full-length pedestal mirror, took a deep breath, unbuttoned the top button of her red sweater, and pulled down the neckline to reveal a deep red scar where her left breast used to be. She had breast cancer. Her battle with the brutal disease had begun several years earlier, when she felt a lump. After a bit of denial, she rushed to her doctor. After that it was mostly a blur—of tests, surgery, doctor's visits, and treatments. But eventually she was patted on the back and pointed toward the door with the instruction to live life to the fullest. It took Alexandra a while to feel like the survivor they labeled her, but after another three months she was on her way to really feeling it, and after another three months she really believed she had made it. But when after almost three years of clean mammograms they found a pea-size lump in her right breast, all the life had fluttered out of her like a punctured balloon.

On this Christmas Eve she was waiting for the results of the biopsy. The doctor's office had assured her that they made test result calls between twelve and three. But somehow she felt sure that they would call only with good news on Christmas Eve; they would wait to call the rest the day after Christmas. She was almost certain she would fall into the latter group. She prayed and cried and wished and cried and cursed and cried. And although she felt completely devoid of hope, something inside of her—maybe just one tiny cell of her—still was holding out for some hope because every day she desperately wished for mail from her grandmother. She had rushed to the mailbox for six days straight with her heart pounding and her throat so dry she was unable to swallow. And each day she walked away from the mailbox in tears.

She looked at herself in the mirror one more time,

then buttoned up her sweater. She was counting her gray hairs when the harsh ringing of the doorbell startled her. She jumped, then waved it off and sat down in the wicker rocking chair. She wasn't expecting anyone and she wasn't going to answer it. Her husband and son were gone until the evening.

Whoever they were, they had no business being there, and she had no use for them. By now all of her family was on their way to her mother's house for Christmas Eve dinner. She would forget the fresh, made-from-scratch vinaigrette and croutons she had made just in case she had a change of heart and decided to not go. She had never missed a Christmas Eve. None of the sisters ever had, but she just didn't think she could do it this year. They wouldn't like it, but they would understand and forgive her. She would probably call at the last minute with some made-up flu story. They wouldn't believe her but would pretend to. The doorbell rang again, then rang again much too quickly. She was annoyed but unmoved. "Whoever it is, they sure are persistent," she grumbled to herself. She was not moving. It rang again. "I am not moving," she said out loud. It rang again. She was becoming exasperated. They were rude and persistent, she thought. When it rang the next time, she swore whoever it was must be lying on the bell.

"Fine," she huffed angrily. "You asked for it!" She stomped down the stairs and angrily flung open the door.

Standing before her was a boy of about twelve dressed in a blue jacket with the word "Vikings" embroidered on it, a gray snow hat, and lumberjack boots. Behind him was a red wagon full of pine wreaths with plaid Christmas bows on them. She glowered at him. His gender and youth prevented him from reading her signals.

"Hey, do you wanna buy one of these Christmas wreaths? I'm selling them for football. We're trying to go to camp this summer." There was a pause, then he said, "I'm Dan from down the street." He said it like he thought it should clinch the deal.

She breathed in a huge gulp of air, not realizing that in her anger she had been holding her breath. "No, I do not want to buy one of your wreaths," she said through gritted teeth. "And I would appreciate you being easier on the doorbell next time." She had expected him to cower, and when he didn't, it took her a bit by surprise.

"Well, I saw the light on," he said. "And I knew you were in there." He wasn't belligerent, he was just twelve. Everything that went through his head came out of his mouth.

"Well, I don't want a wreath," she said again firmly, turning to close the door.

"Why not?" he asked. "Your door's empty."

"Because I don't!" she almost shouted.

"The wreath will die, but you can use the hanger and bow next Christmas."

"I won't be here next Christmas," she blurted. That was the first time she had verbalized her greatest fear, and it almost took her breath away. Even though she knew she would never tell him why she wouldn't be here next year, part of her still wanted him to ask why. But he didn't.

"But you're here now," he said, as if he were pointing out something so obvious that she was stupid for not realizing it herself.

"Excuse me?" she said, starting to resent his tone.

"I said you're here now," he repeated.

"I heard you," she said, her voice rising.

"Then?" he said, raising his palms out in a motion that said "So what's the problem?"

"I won't be here next year and I don't want a wreath," she gritted again.

"Fine," he said. "Don't buy a wreath, lady. Mrs. Pisera always buys two," he grumbled, starting to turn his wagon around. She had her hands on her hips now and was determined to relish her victory by watching him march back down the sidewalk with every single wreath he came up the sidewalk with, but after he took a few steps he turned around.

"Oh, wait," he said with a sour look on his face. "My mom told me to give this to you. It came in our mail. It's not your name, but it is your address." He pulled an envelope from deep within one of his jacket pockets and all but tossed it at her.

She gulped as she reached for it. Her heart raced and her mouth was as dry as sand. It took her eyes a few blinks to focus. It was a letter addressed to her grandmother. She clutched her chest. Her legs were wobbling and her eyes filled with tears.

"Oh, my," she said, holding her hands to her trembling mouth. She let the tears of joy and hope fall. "Thank you," she tried to say, but no sound came out. She looked up; he was halfway down the walk by now.

"Wait!" she croaked. "Wait! Come back!"

He looked at her, annoyed, as if to say "I don't need any more of your grief, lady."

"Come back," she said, trying to sound friendly. "I want to buy one," she called cheerily. "I want to buy a wreath. Wait while I get my purse!" She ran into the house and grabbed her wallet from the entry table.

"I want to buy them all," she squealed, running back to the doorway. She ran too fast and found herself nose to nose with the boy. He just stared at her in the way that only a twelve-year-old boy can. His face said it all. He thought she was completely crazy.

"Don't look at me that way," she said perkily, not really caring at all if he did. "How many do you have?" she asked, pulling bills out of her wallet.

"You don't gotta buy them all, lady," he said, annoyed. "I didn't mean that. You just gotta buy one."

"But I don't want one," she said, her voice way too

happy. "I want them all. I'm sick of Mrs. Pisera's place always looking better than mine. And besides, it's a good investment. I'm going to use the hangers and bow next year too!"

"I thought you weren't going to be here next year," he said flatly.

"Oh, don't be silly," she said. "I'll be here next year."

He shook his head in disgust.

"So how many do you have? Oh, forget it. Here, just take it all. There's more than enough. The rest is for you for being a great little—oops, I mean, a great big salesman."

His eyes were wide. She was definitely out of her mind. He couldn't believe she just called him a great big salesman. He didn't look as if he could take another minute of her.

"Good-bye!" she called happily, watching him rush down the sidewalk. With one last wave she yelled, "Tell your mother I said Merry Christmas." He didn't even turn around. In one swoop she grabbed the huge pile of wreaths that he had dumped on her doorstep and tossed them in the hall. She shut the door with a thud. A flurry of ice crystals followed her into the house.

She took a deep breath and took a long look at the letter. She nodded and laughed out loud, running her fingers over the print of her grandmother's name.

"Thank you, Nunnie," she whispered, looking heavenward. "Thank you." She could feel her presence right then. She could feel her placing a gentle kiss on her cheek.

Alexandra sprang into action. She grabbed her shoes and slid into them, then threw on her coat. She ran to the refrigerator and carefully pulled out the vinaigrette and croutons. Then she slung her purse over her arm and ran out the door. She quickly stuffed the wreaths into the back seat. She didn't want to be late to dinner at her mother's. She was already backing the car out of the driveway when the phone ran. If she had waited just another minute, she would have been in time to hear the good news from her doctor, the good news that she already knew.

ISABELLA

Isabella put on her red sweater coat, wrapped the belt around her waist, and pulled it tight. After she threw her purse over her shoulder, she went to the refrigerator and grabbed the bowl of mandarin oranges that she had left to marinate. She was just taking one last look around the apartment and was about to switch off the light when the phone rang. In an average life, a person answers the phone thousands of times, but only a handful of those calls change a life. This phone call was one of Isabella's handful.

"Oh my! Oh my goodness! Oh, yes! Yes!" she bellowed into the phone. "I'll be right there," she assured emphatically.

"Thank you so much," she squealed. "Can you believe it! On Christmas Eve of all days. Now, this is for sure, right? He will be there, won't he? . . . Right . . . Right. . . . Okay . . . Okay. Thank you. Thank you so much and Merry Christmas."

Later Isabella wouldn't remember most of the drive to the airport. Her mind raced with a million thoughts, but she couldn't recall a single one. She felt excited and scared at the same time. She found a parking spot closer to the terminal than she had expected. She turned off the engine and forced herself to take in a huge gulp of air, trying to calm down. Then she checked her face in the visor mirror and laughed out loud. She put on lipstick anyway, knowing he wouldn't notice or care.

Right then and there she realized that this was a turning point in her life and that when she walked back out of the airport, she would not be the same person that she was when she walked in.

She gently touched the golden cross that was hanging from a chain from the rearview mirror and looked heavenward. She closed her eyes to pray that this was right. In her heart she knew it was, but somehow she needed His affirmation.

"I'm sure everybody is always asking for signs," she whispered. "And I'm sure you're really busy, I mean especially today, but if you wouldn't mind . . ." Her voice trailed off.

She reminded herself that God knew what she

needed before she did, so she probably didn't need to take His time up by going on and on. Besides, she had to go. She hurried into the terminal and felt swallowed up by the maze of activity. There was electricity in the air. It was a happy energy present every day but especially there on Christmas Eve. For the most part, all of the noises mixed smoothly together, then every once in a while there would be an excited squeal followed by joyful laughter. They were the sounds of reunion and love. This was happening all over the building. Bystanders turned to watch the hugging and enjoy the happiness of others. But wasn't that what Christmas was all about?

She checked the arrivals board against the slip of paper on which she had scrawled his flight number. It read ON TIME. She made her way through the crowds and found the gate. Her excitement began to swell again. She was a little early. The rows of seats were mostly empty, except for an elderly gentleman sleeping in one corner seat and a young man wearing an iPod in another.

She chose the first seat in the first row. Settling herself, she stomped a few flakes of snow off her boots, smoothed her sweater, positioned her purse on her lap, and ran her hand through her hair. Then she fixed her eyes on the door. Her concentration lasted only a moment. All of a sudden unsure that she had chosen the perfect seat, she got up and moved three seats to the left. She wiggled herself into place and squinted at the door. Deciding this wasn't the right seat either, she got up again. After another four moves she thought she might have it. But as she stared at the door from her current vantage point, she was losing confidence again.

She was just about to try two seats to the right when a brown-haired woman in a gray furry parka flopped down next to her with a long sigh and a thud. Right away the woman turned to her with a warm smile. "Merry Christmas," she said, blowing her bangs out of her eyes, then crossing her eyes when a stubborn lock floated back down across her face. Isabella laughed. She decided she liked the woman right away.

"Merry Christmas," she greeted back.

"Lisa," she said, introducing herself and offering Isabella her hand.

"Isabella," Isabella said, taking her hand. She thought that Lisa just might be one of those people who carry the Christmas spirit in their heart all year long.

"My son's supposed to be on this flight," Lisa offered, motioning to the door. "Notice," she said, laughing, "I said 'supposed to.' He's in college now and, well, you know. . . ." She laughed, her voice trailing off.

Lisa pulled the collar of her jacket toward Isabella. She was wearing a photo button displaying a nice-looking boy of eighteen or so posing proudly in a basketball uniform.

Isabella smiled. "Handsome," she said.

"Thanks," Lisa said, giving the photo a quick adoring look.

Lisa looked as if she might melt. Lately Isabella had been studying the way that mothers looked at their children. No matter how young or old, no matter how tiny or tall they were, it was always with the most amazing love. Lisa looked back at Isabella with a hopeless gesture.

"He's the love of my life," she said as if to explain it all. "One minute they're little and needing you all the time, and the next they're grown and gone and you're waiting by the phone hoping they return your phone calls. I love that he's independent, but I hate it. College boy," she said with a proud smile. "His name is Matthew." She said his name as if it were the most beautiful word she had ever heard.

"He was so attached when he was little. I used to joke that I walked on the bottoms of my feet and he walked on the tops. He never left my side. Now when he's home, I follow him around the house." Lisa laughed heartily, her eyes focused on the past.

"Once, when he was three, he told me he loved my face." She laughed so hard, tears came to her eyes. "Oh, gosh," she exclaimed. "Listen to me going on and on. I'm such a sap. Enough about me. Who do you have on this flight?"

Isabella blinked. The question stunned her. She sighed and a rush of excitement filled her again. Lisa was waiting for her response. The first time she opened her mouth, no sound came out. She laughed. She tried again.

"My son," she said. "My son is on this flight."

"Oh, great," said Lisa. "I'll get to take a peek at him."

Just then the terminal door slid open.

"OOOOHHH!" Lisa cried as she sprang up from her chair and ran across the room.

She made eye contact with Isabella one last time and waved, beaming as she mouthed the words "Merry Christmas" before she focused expectantly on the doorway. In a moment she had her arms wrapped around a handsome muscular half boy, half man. She was hugging him tightly, rocking back and forth and laughing. The boy was laughing also, with a beautiful mix of embarrassment and joy on his face. He didn't want her to stop. Isabella couldn't help but laugh with them. She was so caught up in their moment that she barely heard the sound of her name being called.

"Isabella Tenley," someone called in a thick accent.

"Oh, oh!" Isabella called back into the thick crowd while fumbling to get her driver's license out of her pocket.

They told her to make sure she had it handy. She tripped through the crowd, craning her neck.

"I'm here!" she called "I'm here. Don't go away." Immediately she realized this was a stupid thing to say. No one was going to travel twenty-five hundred miles to go away after two minutes of searching for someone. She was trying not to panic, but not seeing them was driving her crazy.

"I'm here," she called again.

Suddenly there was a gap in the crowd and she almost fell through it.

"We are here too," called a sweet, accented voice.

Lisa stumbled, catching herself. She looked up, coming face to face with two tiny nuns.

"Hello, Sister—Sisters," she said, trying to smooth her clothes and hair at the same time. The nuns stood calmly, almost serenely, as if they had seen this all before and were just waiting for her to calm down.

"I'm Isabella." She took a deep breath. "I'm Isabella Tenley," she said, her eyes filling with tears.

"I'm Isabella Tenley," she said again softly.

The nuns nodded knowingly. "Yes," they said, nodding back at her. Then together they gently raised the bundle between them. Isabella gasped, holding a hand to her quivering mouth. Tears flowed gently down her cheeks. One of the nuns slowly pulled back one layer of a powder blue blanket to reveal the face of the most beautiful baby boy Isabella had ever seen. She just stared. He was far more beautiful than she had ever dreamed.

"You are mother now," the one sister announced brightly.

"Yes, yes," the other agreed, beginning to untangle herself from the blanket and diaper bag that hung on her shoulder. She hung the bag on Isabella's arm while the other sister handed over the baby.

"You are mother now," the one repeated.

Isabella nodded. "Yes. Yes," she said, laughing. "Thank you. Thank you both very much." The baby was waking and beginning to wriggle beneath the blanket.

"Okay, honey," Isabella said, unwrapping him a bit and straightening him up. He popped his head up turtle-like and raised two chubby arms. In one of his pudgy hands he was holding a small gold cross that hung on a thin, delicate chain.

"He holds them the whole way," the one nun explained.

"Must be for you," the other suggested. Isabella knew these two women were angels.

"Thank you." Isabella nodded. She gently tugged them from his tiny hand. He willingly let them go.

"See?" the smaller of the two chirped.

The baby looked into her eyes and blew bubbles out of his adorable mouth. Isabella laughed out loud. He was amazingly cute.

"Okay," one announced.

"Yes, okay," the other agreed.

Isabella looked up, startled. They were gathering their things. A tiny wave of panic ran through her.

"You are mother now. Merry Christmas," the one said.

"Yes, you are mother now, Merry Christmas."

Stunned, Isabella watched as they each gently planted

a soft kiss on the baby's forehead. Then they turned to her squarely.

"God bless. Good-bye," they said together, then turned away. Isabella stood with her mouth hanging open as she watched them shuffle away, comparing the tickets they held in their hands to the signs above them.

"Thank you," Isabella called after them. They didn't hear her. They melted into the crowd and disappeared.

Isabella took a deep breath. She couldn't believe she was standing there with a baby in her arms. It felt like a dream. She closed her eyes, then opened them again. He was still there and staring very intently back at her.

"Okay," she said, kissing his nose. She loved the way he blinked when she did that.

"It's you and me, baby," she said, trying to calm herself down. She took a deep breath.

"Relax," she said to herself. "We're just like everyone else."

She began to walk out of the airport. Then she corrected herself. "We're *luckier* than everyone else."

Once outside, she shielded him from the wind and the snowflakes. She looked up into the night sky. The baby looked up too. She studied his perfect profile against the black sky. He turned to look at her. He was really seeing her. He studied her face with huge baby eyes. He looked at her as if he had known her all his young life. He was serene and trusting.

"I'm your mama," she told him, pretty sure he already knew this.

"I will love you forever," she added. She said this just in case someday when he was older, he would ask her what her first words to him were.

He made a baby gurgling sound and ever so deliberately raised one finger and carefully guided it to her lips. She closed her eyes, soaking in the moment as she felt his tiny touch. She kissed his finger and said, "Thank you for coming."

One snowflake drifted down from above and landed on top of his tiny eyelash. Isabella had never seen a more beautiful sight. He blinked but it stayed there a moment before melting. The moment was mesmerizing. She wiped tears of gratitude off her face. Looking heavenward, she said, "Thank you." She knew that in that snowflake, she had been given the sign she had asked for.

"Let's get ready to go to Grandma's," she told him. "It's Christmas Eve, you know."

Once in the car, she looked behind her, checking on him. She had spent months looking in that same rearview mirror at the empty car seat. Now it held the love of her life. She smiled and she put the car in reverse, then put on the brakes and shifted back into park. She fished in her pocket and pulled out the tiny gold cross and chain he had just given her. After untangling it, she hung it on the rearview mirror along with hers. She loved the way they looked together.

CHRISTMAS LIGHTS

 One at a time, the cars crept onto St. Martinique Drive. The street had been dusted with crystal-white Christmas Eve snow. The first car arrived at five-forty-five, driven by the chronically early sister. She slid her car into a parking spot and waited for the others. One by one each arrived outside of the red brick, two-story home. Almost on cue, a delicate breeze seemed to blow the snow so that it covered the tracks of each car, leaving the street pristine white after each vehicle parked. The next car arrived five minutes later, found a spot, shut off its engine, and waited. The next two arrived three minutes later, and just a minute after came another. At that point, they were five waiting on the sixth. No one was worried or annoyed. With understanding and patience they waited seven more minutes for the chronically late sister. When she realized she was late as usual, she took the bend in the road a touch more swiftly than the others, parked a little more quickly, then cut her engine. Its clank elicited a collective smile from the five others. Once all of them were there, they began getting out of their vehicles. They took care to shut the doors gently. As was their tradition, they would arrive together, and even though they had been told to come at 6:00 P.M. they still liked to make it a surprise.

With muffled giggles, the six sisters tiptoed up to the doorway of the sixty-year-old house. On the porch they exchanged grand hugs and huge smiles. Every once in a while a delighted squeal would escape, but for the most part they were quiet. They were giddy with the excitement of seeing each other and with the anticipation of the evening that lay before them. Once satisfied that everyone had been greeted and hugged (some twice), they arranged themselves in a group facing the front door.

If one were to go inside of the house and examine the dozens of photographs that were hung on walls, set out on end tables, and pasted into albums, they would realize that they were arranged exactly in the same way in each one that they were now arranged facing the front door.

It was the way their mother had always placed them, so they were trained. In the back row to the far left stood

Isabella, the eldest. Beside her was Alexandra, and next came Victoria. In front of them left to right were Cassandra, Adrianna, and Julianna. Every single one of them had been born in August, six years apart. Their mother preferred to totally devote herself to the first most important six years of a child's life. Then on the month before each one was to enter first grade, she gave birth to the next sister. She said she needed a baby on her hip to help her wave good-bye to the beautiful one who was ready to fly away. She always said she would cry as she watched the school bus drive down the street, but before she reached the front door she had wiped the tears away, inspired by the infant she was holding—her project for the next six years.

And her dedication had paid off, because standing on that porch were six wonderfully adjusted, productive, good women. They had turned out well—actually more than well. They were smart and kind and unique. They were independent and energetic. They loved themselves, each other, and God.

No mother ever anywhere had put more into their children than their mother had put into them. She was an educator and mother through and through. She filled their days with reading and writing, literature and science, music and the arts of every kind. They learned, exploring and creating freely. They were taught to be smart but, just as much, they were taught to be kind. They took care of themselves but served others and the community by picking up litter and baking muffins for elderly neighbors. They planted gardens and shoveled snow. They sang and danced and prayed.

Their mother had given them regal names. They were beautiful yet smart names. In its proper form, each name was both unique and a mouthful to say, flowery yet intelligent. No one was named for a season or emotion (no Summer or Joy). No one was named for a color or a flower (no Amber or Rose). No one was named for a month or a city (no April or Savannah).

Standing before the front door were Isabella, Victoria, Cassandra, Alexandra, Adrianna, and Julianna.

In front of the door they giggled and adjusted themselves one last time; then, as was the tradition, they let Julianna, the youngest, ring the bell. "The baby of the family is in charge of all buttons and bells," their mother had always said. And since no one came after Julianna, the job was hers forever.

Within moments of the first chime, the most beautiful woman any of them had ever seen, their mother, opened the door. Each one's heart leapt and warmed in a unique yet similar way. Silent no more, they squealed with excitement, delight, and love. They each flung themselves at her, hugging her with all their might.

They were no longer Isabella, Victoria, Alexandra, Cassandra, Adrianna, and Julianna. When they crossed this doorway they became Izzy, Tori, Allie, Cassie, Addie, and Julie.

They rushed into the house, filling it with life. In a flurry coats and parkas were torn off and hung up. Christmas presents were hurriedly placed under the Christmas tree. Lights were dimmed. Candles were lit in the old Italian-style dining room. The table was already set and dressed with a rich red table cloth and matching napkins. China that once graced their parents' wedding tables now lay on this table. Julianna placed a large gold bowl with fresh salad greens in the center. Before taking a seat, each daughter deposited her contribution. Izzy tossed in the oranges, Tori the celery, Addie the cranberries, Cassie the almonds. Their mother appeared from the kitchen with warm pecan-crusted salmon and laid it on top. Allie finished it off with the dressing, then gave it a stir. Each took the seat that she had taken since childhood. Each wore a red sweater bought by their mother. Each one's cheeks were flushed with excitement as she settled into her chair. They watched silently as their mother took her place at the head of the table. They waited expectantly. The mother raised her cup of tea, looked them in the eyes, and softly said "Merry Christmas, my loves."

With misty eyes they softly answered, "Merry Christmas, Mom."

She cleared her throat. "Let's begin," she said, "like

we should begin all things—with a prayer." Lovingly, they joined hands and bowed their heads.

"Dear Lord," she began. "Let us first thank you for the gift of your love and the gift of each other. We thank you for returning us all back here safely again this year. We hope that how we have spent this past year pleases you. We're sorry for the wrongs we have done and we ask for your forgiveness. And we ask you for your continued blessing. Amen."

"Amen," they repeated.

They giggled as the party began. The mother checked her watch. They all knew why; they had only one hour to themselves. In one hour the rest of the family—the husbands, children, boyfriends, and significant others—would arrive. But the first hour of each Christmas Eve belonged to them. It was sacred.

The chatting and giggling began slowly then quickened, rolling over them like soothing warm ocean waves.

The mother sat back in her seat and relaxed. Her daughters followed suit. They waited. She scanned the table.

Then, beginning a game that she had played with them since childhood, she said, "Hello, Isabella. How are you?"

Isabella giggled like the little girl that she hadn't been in years.

"I'm good, Mom." She blushed.

"Tell me something that will make me smile?"

Izzy giggled again. "Well," she began, her face coloring a bit. The others' curiosity was growing because Izzy never blushed. With everyone's attention focused on her, she began again. But this time when she opened her mouth, no sound came out. So unlike her to be at a loss for words or flustered, the others were busting with the anticipation.

"I'm waiting, Isabella," the mother joked. This and the laughter of the sisters broke the tension.

This time when she spoke, her words came out in a rush.

"I've found someone," she blurted. A collective gasp filled the room. Eyes were wide. They all knew that Isabella probably had hoped to find someone to share her life with someday. Who didn't, after all? But time passed and it never happened. Isabella, one of the more private sisters, didn't wear her heart on her sleeve. They assumed the desire might still be there, but it just was not talked about. Isabella was more of the solver of her younger sisters' problems than she was the one lamenting her own. She was in her forties now, so they thought maybe that the stage had passed. But sitting there at that table with their mouths hanging open they realized it hadn't. A few of them stammered bits of questions, not knowing where to begin.

"Well," Isabella began, "he's amazing."

"How long have you known him?" a sister asked.

"Not long," said Izzy matter-of-factly. "But it's true what they say," she gushed. "I knew the moment I saw him that he was the one. Definitely love at first sight." She was playing with them now. They squealed in excitement. Addie clapped; she always clapped when she was excited.

"What does he look like?"

"Yeah, what does he look like?"

They were starving for the details.

"Well," Isabella began, truly enjoying herself now. "He's got silky black hair and the most amazing eyes."

"Is he tall?"

"No," Izzy said. "He isn't, but I'm okay with it. He's a little pudgy too, but I'm okay with that too."

They all nodded supportively. Looks meant nothing. Just when Izzy thought she might be losing their attention, she reached into her purse and said, "I do have a picture."

"Oh, Isabella! For goodness sakes," one of them admonished as the others joined in. "We could have started with the picture!"

Isabella teased them one last time, gazing lovingly at the photo in her hand.

"Hand it over," Cassie ordered. Of course Isabella handed the photo to her mother first. Her mother studied the photo and blinked, tears of understanding pooling in her eyes. She took her daughter's hand and kissed it. "He's simply beautiful."

A tear fell from Isabella's eyes. "Thanks, Mommy."

"You will be wonderful," her mother stated. Those words meant the world to Isabella. She nodded, unable to speak.

The sisters were confused but only momentarily. Complete understanding enveloped them as they viewed the picture of their new nephew, Isabella's adoptive son.

"When did you get him?" someone asked incredulously.

"I just picked him up today," she joked matter-of-factly. "Right after I picked up the oranges for the salad." Laughter filled the room.

"Good girl, Isabella," the mother said.

Izzy basked in the praise. "Thanks, Mom."

"Congratulations, Izzy," Victoria said, raising her teacup.

"To Izzy," they said together.

"To Izzy and—" Cassie stopped as he realized they didn't know the baby's name.

"Yeah. Isabella, what's his name?" they asked.

Izzy smiled. "It's Joseph, of course," she said softly. Joseph was their father's name. A hint of sadness glimmered in each woman's eyes. Silence surrounded them for a moment, then their mother broke the silence with a gentle authority that they all recognized. Wallowing in sadness had never been allowed. "It's unbecoming," she had always told them.

She cleared her throat.

"Speaking of your father," she began, "he's doing well, and says hello and Merry Christmas to all of you." After a pause she added, "And of course he wants you to know that he misses and loves you all very much."

They nodded, their heads down. They admired her strength, courage, and faith even if they couldn't quite relate to it. Secretly they each wondered if one day they might be called to face the same challenge their mother was facing. But as always, their mother was a model for them.

"Really," she insisted brightly, her voice light. "He is fine. You can't be married to a man for fifty years and not know when he's fine and when he isn't and what he's thinking.

"Actually," she added, "I made him a quilt this year for Christmas and he loved it. He was using it when I left him today."

They nodded again in agreement, admiring her strength.

"So then," she began, signaling that they were moving on. She scanned the table. Like little girls, they giggled, squirming in their seats. Before she could choose one of them, Julianna offered herself with a shy wave of her hand.

"Maybe I should be next," she said self-consciously.

They all laughed. Of all the sisters, this game was probably the most difficult for Julianna. Being the youngest, she always felt herself so many steps behind the others. She really wasn't sure why, but somehow it all seemed to embarrass her.

To Julianna, her sisters' lives seemed complete and put together while her own life seemed to be taking forever to get started.

"Great," her mother said encouragingly. "Tell me something that will make me smile."

The eyes of her big sisters were on her. They were patient and kind eyes, eyes that truly cared. She was everyone's baby.

"It's nothing really," Julianna began with the genuine embarrassment of a teenager.

"If it's something to you, then it's something to us," Isabella pointed out. They all nodded in agreement, willing her to go on. No one said a word; each sister was afraid that she might retreat back into a hole like a frightened bunny. They all had had their turn being the awkward teenager, and they knew how hard it was.

"It's just . . ." she began, then suddenly she lost her nerve and bowed her head. They waited.

"It's that someone likes me," she blurted out. Still there was silence. She looked up; they were waiting for more. They didn't understand. But there wasn't any more. Julianna sighed, then said it again. "Someone likes me, *likes* me," she repeated with the emphasis on "likes" this time.

All of a sudden a rush of understanding crashed down and a collective "OOOOOOOOOOOOOH" filled the room. They hadn't meant to do it. It's just that they were so excited for her. But having meant it or not, they lost her. She was embarrassed beyond repair and was now sitting with her knees drawn up to her chest and her red face buried in her arms. They laughed at her lovingly. She looked so cute to them.

"Tell us about him?" Alexandra asked.

She did not answer; instead, they watched as she nodded her head, still in her arms, back and forth. Again they laughed.

"At least tell us his name," Isabella said.

Again a nod and more laughter.

"Okay, okay," Victoria said, attempting a compromise. "Just tell us if you like him, like him back."

They were silent. This was a good question.

They waited. For a moment nothing happened. Then slowly Julianna uncurled one arm from around her head, leaving the other to still hide her face.

They watched with anticipation as she straightened her arm. They collectively held their breath, then broke into cheers of delight as she gave them one thumb up.

Her mother looked amused. "Good things come to those who pray," she reminded. "Good girl, Julianna."

A muffled "Thanks, Mom" came from beneath the arms. With one more laugh they moved on.

The mother scanned the table waiting for a volunteer, not expecting the one she got. Victoria put her hand up shyly. It was known that this was not Victoria's favorite game either. Her straightforward doctor's personality made it easy for her to talk about the "facts" of things, but the "feelings" of things were not quite as easy to talk about.

"Well, this is a surprise." The mother laughed, raising a playful eyebrow that made the others laugh too.

Victoria could feel her cheeks color. Her sisters looked at their mother. The mother faced Victoria. "Hello, Victoria," she said. The girls giggled. "Tell me something that will make me smile."

"Okay." She laughed, butterflies dancing in her stomach. She might as well get it over with. There never was and never would be hiding anything from her sisters or mother. She swallowed and decided just to jump in and say it. And if she wasn't so sure about what she had felt that afternoon, she would never tell them, but she *was* sure. She always wondered what all the fuss about love was. Now she knew.

"I think maybe I might have found someone too," she managed.

There was a collective cheer amid the clapping. Of all of them, no one tried less to attract a man than Tori did. It was actually one of their jokes. They would say, "If Tori were to end up married, a man would have to drop down at her feet in the middle of a church already dressed in a tuxedo with a ring in his hand." Little did they know that he arrived dressed in scrubs next to her balcony with Baby Jesus in his hand.

"Since earlier today?" her mother asked jokingly.

"You told me to try," Tori responded weakly in her own defense.

This amused her mother, who chuckled heartily.

"I knew it would happen to you!" Cassie insisted gleefully. "No matter how hard you tried to avoid it!"

"Wait," Isabella said, silencing the playful racket. "He is over twenty-six inches tall, isn't he?" They roared with laughter.

Victoria nodded, laughingly assuring them that he indeed was.

"When did you meet?" Cassandra asked.

"Today." She shrugged. This caused laughter.

"Where?"

"My balcony." This caused more laughter.

"You found him on your balcony?" They were howling now. She nodded again.

"Too bad you don't have a picture," someone said.

The look on Victoria's face gave her away. Truly a cat that swallowed the canary.

"Hand it over!" Izzy ordered.

Without much of a protest, she reached into her purse for her camera phone.

"Your camera phone, Tori! How tacky!" one sister joked.

"How clever," their mother corrected with a wink. Tori clicked the buttons to make the picture she had sneakily taken earlier appear, then handed it to them.

She watched their faces as they passed it around the table. They cooed in approval.

"Leave it to you!" Izzy muttered in mock disgust. "To end up with that without even trying!"

"He *is* gorgeous," Allie remarked.

Automatically Tori thanked them, then became self-conscious that she assumed he was hers, but her heart told her that he was.

"Hey," Adrianna said, taking one last look at the photo before handing the phone back. "The nativity scene Mom bought you is in the background."

Their mother smiled in approval. "Good girl, Victoria."

Those words always felt so good.

"Thanks, Mom," she said, allowing her mind to drift back to the afternoon.

The mother raised her eyebrows jokingly. "Any volunteers?" For a moment nothing, then Allie raised a hand.

"Me," she squeaked.

"Hello, Alexandra," the mother said.

"Hi, Mom," she answered lovingly.

"Tell me something that will make me smile."

Allie nodded. "I think—" she began, then she corrected herself. "I *know* I'm going to be okay." It felt good to say it out loud; saying it somehow made it more real. But it was a bold thing for her to say.

Her mother nodded, as did all of her sisters.

No one asked why, even though they wanted to know where she had found her faith. They gave her time. Allie looked down at her hands and collected herself before she began again. She knew they were wondering.

"Did you hear from your doctor?" Victoria managed timidly. Allie shook her head no, then gathered the courage to begin again. She decided that blurting it out would be best.

"I heard from Grandma," she explained, making cautious eye contact with her family.

There was a collective pause, then smiles crossed each face and they laughed gently.

Allie shrugged. "Grandma won a trip to Aruba," she finally confessed. The gentle laughter turned into a roar.

That was all any of them needed. They looked at their sister with loving eyes. To them she was heroic. Her battle with breast cancer had been devastating. They had prayed her well.

"We all know you are going to be just fine," the mother said firmly.

"You will," each of them repeated.

Feeling the warmth of their love, Allie could only nod back.

The mother started to go on, then, suddenly remembering, Allie jumped in. "Wait," she said. "I bought a wreath for each of you from some kid in the neighborhood. They're in my car."

"Great," they all said.

"Good girl, Alexandra," said the mother.

"Thanks, Mom," she answered.

They waited to see who would be chosen next. They were down to the last two sisters.

"How about you, Adrianna?" the mother asked. "How are you?"

"Fine, Mom." Addie blushed.

Her mother winked playfully at her. "Tell me something that will make me smile."

"Okay," Adrianna began, not really sure herself where she was going with this or how she was going to explain it. The mother and sisters waited patiently. Sometimes it took Addie time to organize her thoughts.

Addie was the shy sister, the traditional one, much more conservative than any of the others. She lacked the spunk that the others had but had a beautiful softness about her that maybe they lacked. Addie was a peacemaker—possibly to a fault. Because of their great love for her, Addie was the cause of some worry for her sisters. Some people just seemed too sweet for this world. But Addie always assured them that she was happy being herself and the world would not swallow her whole.

"*Softer*, not weaker," her mother reminded her sisters when they voiced their concern. Their mother often shared private winks with Addie. And in those winks was the message of unconditional love from mother to daughter, a message that said "You are beautiful just the way you are." But in more private moments, the mother would assure her, "If you choose to stand up for yourself, that would be okay too." A memory they all shared was one of Addie in first grade.

Every day of first grade the mother packed Addie's lunch with a chocolate cupcake. And every day Karen Kyler, her unkind classmate, would demand the cupcake, and Addie would hand it over. And every night the mother would discuss the situation with Addie at the kitchen table, holding her tiny hands in hers. They spoke in whispers. From the youngest ages the mother spoke to them as adults, took their problems seriously. Night after night they sat together. Addie would explain that Karen had taken the cupcake. Each night the mother would ask her what she thought they should do to solve the problem, and each night sitting there in her cloud pajamas with her bare feet hanging from the chair, Addie would shrug her shoulders and say that she didn't know. The mother would kiss her on the forehead and send her to bed. The other sisters certainly had their opinions—everything from smashing the cupcake into nasty Karen's face to punching her squarely in the nose. But one night from the warmth and safety of her loving home Addie said she thought she had figured it out. Her mother sat down next to her, giving her daughter not only her complete attention but her complete respect.

Her mother waited. Finally Addie spoke softly yet decisively. "I think I should bring a vanilla cupcake—Karen doesn't like vanilla."

The mother nodded, kissed Addie on the forehead, took a vanilla cupcake from the cupboard, placed it in her lunchbox, and sent her to bed.

"You truly are a peacemaker, Adrianna," their mother said. "And you know what they say: 'Blessed are the peacemakers.' "

All eyes were glued to Addie.

"I stood up to Ron," she finally said. There was silence. No one dared to touch this one. They deferred to their mother as to what to say on the outside, but on the inside, each was wildly cheering her on.

"So you stood up to Ron?" the mother repeated without emotion.

Addie nodded.

"We love him, dear, but maybe he does need a little standing up to," their mother, forever the diplomat, said.

The sisters nodded in agreement, trying not to make their pleasure so obvious. They had felt that Ron needed standing up to for a while and more than a few times had offered to do it for her.

"I stood up to him . . . and he apologized."

"Go, Addie!!" Victoria cheered. "Ooops. Sorry."

Adrianna laughed. "That's okay. I think it might have made things better," she said self-consciously. This kind of thing was difficult for her. She knew how her sisters felt. That maybe she should stick up for herself a bit more. That maybe they didn't like Ron quite so much. But . . .

"I think it might make things better too," the mother gently assured her. She reached over and touched her daughter's hand. They exchanged a look—a look from a mother that told her daughter that she loved her just the way she was.

"Good girl," the mother said to her ever so softly.

"Thank you," Addie mouthed back.

"Hey, just for the fun of it," Isabella teased, "just how surprised was Ron?"

Addie giggled. "Very."

"Works for me," Isabella joked. They let themselves laugh. Someone ruffled Addie's hair.

The mother said "Well, who's left?" Scanning the table, her gaze fell upon Cassie. She allowed her eyes a glint of sadness.

"I am," Cassie offered, willing her voice to sound cheerful and perky. Instead it came out sounding more like a croak. The others ignored it and Cassie tried again.

"Hello, Cassandra," the mother said. "Tell me something that will make me smile."

Cassie nodded and gulped and willed her voice strong. "Well," she began. The room was silent except for the gentle clanging of a fork against a dish or a spoon grazing the side of a teacup. Cassie looked back at them and wished their eyes didn't look so sad. It made her feel pathetic, which in some ways she was, but less so these days than others. But she knew it was love and concern in their eyes, and she loved them back for it.

"I'm doing well," she said. They responded with unsure, weak smiles and nods.

"Really," she said. "I—" she began. It was a sentence that she wasn't sure she should have started or should even continue. It was like verbalizing your deepest darkest secret. Admitting it to herself was difficult enough. Saying it out loud was frightening.

"I'm doing well," she repeated.

"I find him in things," she said, waiting for their

responses. Would they think she was crazy? That was her biggest fear. But they didn't react; they just listened. She took in some air and began again.

"I find him in things," she explained. She struggled for just the right words. "Like . . . like . . . like smells . . . like oranges. He loved oranges." She gulped as her eyes filled with tears. She had gathered the courage to go this far and she wasn't going to turn back. "I find him in sunsets and clouds—it's corny, I know, but I do. I find him when I hear trains. Remember how he loved trains? So I find him in things," she said, her voice quivering. "And it makes it a little okay."

They were nodding now with tears streaming down their faces. They understood. They did not think she was crazy. They thought she was amazing.

"I sat for a while in his room today," she said. "And I felt him—and it helps—it makes me a little stronger." She was crying now, but it was okay. She bowed her head. She was done.

"Good for you, Cassie," Tori said.

"Yeah, really good for you, Cass," Isabella said.

The others joined in nodding with chirps of encouragement.

"Good girl," the mother said. "Good girl, Cassandra."

"Thanks, Mom" she said, wiping her face dry. She was okay.

They relaxed in the moment. One by one they joined hands. The candles had burned down to provide the perfect golden flickering glow. They were warmed by the fireplace as well as by the overwhelming love that filled the room. They knew how lucky they were. They wanted to bask in it for just a moment.

The mother checked her watch. It was a signal to them. With each girl doing her part, they cleared the table of dishes, leaving only a twenty-inch evergreen tree in the center. Their time alone was almost over for another year.

"Well," the mother said, smiling lovingly at them. "It certainly seems as if you have all been busy and that you have all been well. You have been smart and strong and good. You have done for yourselves but done more for others. It seems as if you have loved and laughed . . . It seems that you have made me proud. It seems that you have made me smile."

Her daughters surrounded her.

"Good girls," she said.

And without any more words, the mother handed each a red satin box. The boxes were well taken care of but showed their age with their faded color and fraying edges.

Each daughter silently and very carefully opened her box, reached inside, and pulled out its contents. Peeling off the red tissue paper, each revealed a delicate white

Christmas bulb bearing a baby picture of herself. On the back of each bulb was a switch. One by one each daughter turned her bulb on, illuminating it with a warm, soft glow. They couldn't help but smile at the images of themselves from long ago. The mother turned off the dining room lights and one by one, beginning with Izzy down to Julie, they took their turns placing their bulb on the tree until it held six glowing bulbs. It stood looking beautiful.

They joined hands to pray. With hearts swelling with love, feeling God's grace, they prayed. "Our Father, who art in heaven, hallowed be thy name. Thy kingdom come, thy will be done, on earth as it is in heaven. Give us this day our daily bread and forgive us our trespasses as we forgive those who trespass against us and lead us not into temptation but deliver us from evil."

Together they said, "Amen."

With just a moment left, they paused and faced their mother and waited for her to say it. And because it was tradition, she did. She said, "Every day you are the lights of my life. But today, my loves, you are my Christmas lights."

There was just enough time for each to have one more teary-eyed hug before the doorbell rang announcing the arrival of the others.

CHRISTMAS LIGHTS PECAN-CRUSTED SALMON SALAD WITH ORANGE-TARRAGON VINAIGRETTE

Serves 8

8 three-ounce portions boneless, skinless salmon

2 cups clover honey

2 cups coarsely ground pecans

VINAIGRETTE

½ cup orange juice

½ cup apple cider vinegar

¼ cup granulated sugar

2 tablespoons minced shallot

2 tablespoons minced fresh tarragon

2 cups olive oil

Salt and pepper

CHRISTINE PISERA NAMAN

SALAD MIX

   2 heads romaine lettuce, chopped

   1 pound fresh field greens

   1 cup diced celery (approximately ¼ inch)

   2 cups canned mandarin oranges, drained

   1 cup dried cranberries

   1 cup sliced toasted almonds

Preheat oven to 350°F. Coat salmon portions on one side with honey, then dip into ground pecans, preferably not skin side. Place portions, coated sides facing up, on a buttered or oiled cookie sheet (vegetable spray may be substituted). Bake for 12 minutes.

Meanwhile, combine all vinaigrette ingredients except the olive oil and salt and pepper in a blender or food processor and blend. Add the olive oil in a steady flow, ½ cup at a time, so dressing emulsifies. Add salt and pepper to taste.

Combine the salad mix ingredients in a large mixing bowl. (Extra mandarin orange slices, almonds, and cranberries may be reserved for garnish, if desired.) Toss with the vinaigrette and divide among individual plates. Top with the salmon, garnish, and serve. Salmon may be served hot, cold, or at room temperature.

Recipe created by Chef Rocco Frank Pisera

Mattituck-Laurel Library